Totally 1

Sure Mastery
Unsure
Sure Thing
Surefire

Re-Awakening
The Three R's

Sure Mastery

SUREFIRE

ASHE BARKER

Surefire
ISBN # 978-1-78184-726-8
©Copyright Ashe Barker 2014
Cover Art by Posh Gosh ©Copyright January 2014
Interior text design by Claire Siemaszkiewicz
Totally Bound Publishing

This is a work of fiction. All characters, places and events are from the author's imagination and should not be confused with fact. Any resemblance to persons, living or dead, events or places is purely coincidental.

All rights reserved. No part of this publication may be reproduced in any material form, whether by printing, photocopying, scanning or otherwise without the written permission of the publisher, Totally Bound Publishing.

Applications should be addressed in the first instance, in writing, to Totally Bound Publishing. Unauthorised or restricted acts in relation to this publication may result in civil proceedings and/or criminal prosecution.

The author and illustrator have asserted their respective rights under the Copyright Designs and Patents Acts 1988 (as amended) to be identified as the author of this book and illustrator of the artwork.

Published in 2014 by Totally Bound Publishing, Newland House, The Point, Weaver Road, Lincoln, LN6 3QN, United Kingdom.

No part of this book may be reproduced, scanned, or distributed in any printed or electronic form without permission. Please do not participate in or encourage piracy of copyrighted materials in violation of the authors' rights. Purchase only authorised copies.

Totally Bound Publishing is an imprint of Total-E-Ntwined Limited.

If you purchased this book without a cover you should be aware that this book is stolen property. It was reported as "unsold and destroyed" to the publisher and neither the author nor the publisher has received any payment for this "stripped book".

SUREFIRE

Dedication

This book is dedicated to my family, as ever, John, Hannah and Jack.

Chapter One

"Eva! You mean Eva Eva?" Eloquent, that's me.

Tom too, it would seem. "Yes, Eva Eva. Nathan's Eva. And she's not on her own."

Just the mysterious Eva materializing out of nowhere was enough to floor me. And by the sound of it, Tom was every bit as surprised. But there's more apparently. He's not volunteering so I have to ask. "So, who else is with her?"

"Her baby."

"Her..." Words do fail me now. I'm scurrying across the yard toward my car and I manage to drop my phone. By the time I've retrieved it from under my rear tire, the obvious inference has occurred to me. "The baby, is it...? I mean... How old is it? The baby?"

"About ten weeks I gather. And yes, she's Nathan's baby."

"Ah." Says it all really. Complicated doesn't come close to describing this. Still, I've always had the distinct impression Nathan Darke likes children. I'm just wondering whether or not to offer up that optimistic observation when Tom's voice cuts through my tangled thoughts again.

"We could really do with a bit more time here, before Rosie arrives back and everything gets messy again."

Again?

"Nathan needs time to talk to Eva, and I'm on my way to Keighley to get hold of a cot. Grace is babysitting, so that leaves you. Could you think up some delaying tactic, take Rosie for a burger or something, just keep her out for an extra hour or so?"

"Yes, I daresay I could. Won't she think it a bit odd though, me just turning up? I never meet her from school."

"Maybe, but she'll be so delighted to see you she'll soon forget."

"I take it I'm not telling her about Eva or the baby?"

"I think that's down to Nathan. Just hedge as best you can until you get back here. And, Ashley, I do appreciate this, babe. Nathan does too."

"I— You're welcome. I'll see you in a couple of hours or so then." And I hang up, get the car started then I'm off, headed for Rosie's school.

* * * *

She was surprised to see me hanging round the school gate, and just as delighted as Tom thought she'd be. Amazingly, she never once asked where Grace or her dad were, just accepting me as part of the family team. It's a fairly warm, fuzzy sort of a feeling, I decide, being part of a family again—a family who looks out for each other and rally around to help in a crisis. I'm mulling that over and responding to Rosie's excited chatter as we tootle along the road heading for

McDonalds in Keighley. She's full of stories about her day, the painting of Barney she's half finished, the 'Cat in the Hat' poem her teacher read to the class and the particularly disgusting fish that was on offer in the school dinner hall. A less than enjoyable lunch seems like a good excuse to pig out on a Big Mac before we head for home, and Rosie buys that suggestion enthusiastically. So far so good.

An hour later we're pushing the empty wrappers and cartons around on the bright red plastic tray, and I'm wondering if it might be all right to head for home when my phone buzzes to signal the arrival of a text. I send Rosie to dump our debris in the huge bin while I check it.

Fine to come home. See you soon. Love you. T

Sounds promising. I smile, especially at the last bit. My response is short—

On our way. 20 mins. Love you too. A

Knowing what we'll be walking into makes the short ride home rather fraught for me, but Rosie seems oblivious to any tension, or to my general silence. I pull up at the huge gate into Black Combe and Rosie hops out to press the buzzer. A few seconds, then the massive gate slides majestically aside, and Rosie skips alongside the car as I crunch over the gravel toward the house. I navigate the bend in the drive and the house comes into view, Nathan's sleek black Porsche parked in front. I pull up alongside as Rosie fusses with an excited Barney bouncing around the house to greet us. I get out of the car and, flanked by Rosie and Barney, stroll around to the kitchen door at the back.

Rosie flings it open when we get there, bounces inside full of news of horrible fish and delightful chicken nuggets and strawberry McFlurries. I follow more cautiously, not entirely sure what sight might greet us.

What we get is a surreal spin on domestic bliss. Rosie comes skidding to a halt, her excited stream of girlish babble silenced at the sight of her father seated at the kitchen table, a tiny baby in his arms sucking contentedly from a bottle of milk. She stares at him, astonished, then at the baby—a remarkably pretty little thing, incidentally, all pink and fragrant. Her eyes are closed, the very picture of contentment, and her cheeks are moving rhythmically, suckling the bottle. The tiny air bubbles rising through the milk indicate her success, and Nathan tilts it to improve the angle for her. The adoration in his gaze is unmistakable. Clearly, Rosie has a sister.

Not that she knows it yet, and I'm wondering if I should make myself scarce, give him the space to talk to her alone. Apparently not.

"Hi, you two. Rosie, come over here, there's someone you need to meet. Ashley, my hands are full. You don't mind making your own coffee do you? Mine's black."

He gestures with his head to the empty chair next to him, and Rosie scurries across the kitchen.

"Uh, no. Not at all…" I set about fixing us both a coffee.

"Whose baby is it? Can I hold her? What's her name? How long are we looking after her for? Does she like Barbies?" Rosie seems to have rallied admirably from her surprise and is bombarding Nathan with questions.

The excited babble cuts off suddenly as Rosie spots something else, something equally incongruous to her.

And I confess I'm also a little puzzled by the presence of the rather battered violin case occupying pride of place on the kitchen table. Rosie stares at it for a few moments then turns to her father, with her eyes wide and mouth quivering.

"That's Eva's. Eva's violin. She took it with her. But it's here again. Why is it here, Daddy?"

"Hush, love. Listen to me." He hesitates, his gaze fastened on Rosie's excited, hopeful little face, then he hits her with the big one. "Eva brought it. She's back. She's upstairs, asleep."

Rosie leaps to her feet, obviously intending to bolt for the stairs to see for herself the beloved Eva, truly returned from…wherever.

"Rosie, wait. Come back here, sit down and listen to me. Now, please."

Nathan's voice stops her mad rush. Rosie does as she's been told, as anyone would, I suspect, on hearing that tone, and he continues. "Eva's here, you'll see her soon. But she's been poorly, and now she's tired so she's asleep. We need to let her have a good, long rest, and you can talk to her later, I promise. The doctor needs to come and see her as well."

He nods his thanks to me as I place a mug of black coffee on the table in front of him, then he turns again to Rosie. "This is Isabella. She's Eva's baby." He smiles at Rosie's wide-eyed, astonished look and goes on, "And mine. She's your baby sister."

Rosie looks from him to me then back again, searching our faces for some sign that this could make sense. That baby sisters do just turn up out of the blue, and can be found waiting for you in the kitchen when you come home from school. No one speaks. By common, unspoken consent we all let the silence stretch as each of us, I suppose, assimilates the impact of the day's events.

Then, "Is she staying? I mean, are they both staying? Daddy, please don't let her go away again. Please…" Rosie's eyes are tearful now, her lips quivering again as she considers the prospect of losing her—well, I don't exactly know what Eva is to Rosie, but she's clearly very important—all over again.

It's clear to me that although she likes me well enough, I'm her friend, maybe even a bit like a big sister. But Eva? Now Eva's something very special to Rosie. And I suspect to Nathan too. I hope for all their sakes this is going to turn out okay.

Nathan's voice is gentle as he tries to reassure her, but of course, there are no guarantees. Not yet at least. "I hope so, love. I'm going to try my very best to persuade her."

The clatter of footsteps along the hallway announces the arrival of Tom and Grace. Tom strolls into the kitchen, smiles at me and drops a quick kiss on the top of my head. "Thanks for helping out, love. Nice burger, sprout?" He ruffles Rosie's hair as she turns to him, her tears forgotten and her eyes now sparkling with excitement again.

"I had chicken nuggets. But Tom, Tom, we've got a baby. Me and Daddy. And Eva. Eva's upstairs. She's called Isabella and she's my sister."

Tom smiles back at her. "Yeah, so I hear. You gonna help look after her then? That's what big sisters do."

"Yes. I'll help. I can brush her hair and read books to her. And show her where the tadpoles are, and…" She stops, more than certainly to think what else might need to go in her job description while Nathan smiles down at both his daughters. And I don't think I've ever seen a man look more delighted with life. Or more torn.

Tom shakes his head, clearly impressed at this display of sisterly diligence. "Sounds like you'll be busy, sprout. I hope you'll still have time to come and help me with the baby piglets from time to time." He turns to Nathan. "Looks like you've picked up the core skills pretty quick. Anyway, the cot's assembled and on the landing, not sure which room you want it in so..."

"No problem. Thanks, mate, I appreciate what you've done today."

"Any time, my friend. Any time." And, turning to me, "So, gorgeous, can you give me a lift home then? When you've finished your coffee — no rush."

* * * *

Twenty minutes later we're cruising along the lane headed for Greystones, and I've had the rest of the tale from Tom. It seems they finished their meetings in Preston earlier than they expected and were headed back to Black Combe in Nathan's Porsche. They were almost home when a Mini — Eva's car — came swerving around the bend in the road, just before the turnoff up to Black Combe. Nathan swerved to avoid hitting it, and Eva lost control of her car. Next thing she was upside down in the tarn and sinking under about eight feet of water. As the Mini had shot past them Tom had seen Eva at the wheel, although he thought Nathan had recognized the car before, as soon as it had appeared. According to Tom, Nathan had more or less stood the Porsche on its nose, and he was out of his car and into the water after her like a man possessed. Luckily he's a good swimmer, a scuba diver in fact, and he was able to get down there and get her out of the car in time. A few seconds later, and I doubt she'd have made it. It was a close thing, but she's alive, and apparently sleeping it all off in Nathan's bed. But the really odd thing is the baby wasn't in the car with her. She'd apparently already been up to Black Combe and had just left Isabella with Grace, announced she was Nathan's baby and that he could have her. Next thing she's hurtling down the road, taking corners too fast and driving into the lake.

"It all sounds really odd. She just left her baby behind?" Given my history that's especially difficult for me to understand, but who am I to judge?

"Yeah, that's what Grace said. And that she was very, very upset. Distraught is how Grace describes it and she thinks Eva might have, well, that she might have done it deliberately. Tried to kill herself."

I turn to him, dismayed. Not good, so not good. "Shit. What does Nathan think?"

"His gut reaction's that it was an accident. Mine too, if I'm honest. She looked to me, in that split second as her Mini skidded past us, like she was trying to stop, trying to brake. She was just going too bloody fast, but I don't think she intended to end up in the lake. He'll talk to her though, when she wakes up. See what she has to say."

"Right." Then, for the want of something more incisive, "Shit."

* * * *

It *was* an accident. We all know that now. Eva was ill, totally pole-axed by post-natal depression. She'd struggled since Isabella had been a few days old, and had come back to Nathan in sheer desperation. She needed help, and she found it at Black Combe. A bit like I did, I suppose.

Eva's a couple of years older than me, and we have absolutely nothing in common, apart from our fatal attraction to Dominant men perhaps. In fact, she's the sort of girl I always avoided at school. The brainy types, the ones who did their homework, got awarded achievement prizes at Speech Day and never got detentions. Those girls always intimidated me, if I'm honest, and when I learnt that Eva's a doctor of something not medical, speaks about twenty different languages, has degrees in music, maths, languages, and God knows what else, I just wanted to crawl under a stone. No way was dull, ordinary little Ashley McAllister ever going to be able to compare to that glittering career, that litany of achievements. Or so I thought. Then Eva turned out to be nice, and that confused me. She *is* clever, a gifted musician. But just plain nice too. And she's just as shy as me, just as unsure of herself, and of her welcome here.

So, I've put my prejudices to one side and we've become friends. She likes my pictures, I like to listen to her play the violin. But then, who wouldn't?

The first time I met Eva, actually met her, she'd been back at Black Combe for about three weeks. For the first two weeks she never came out of her—their—bedroom as far as I could tell. I continued to call at Black Combe most mornings to collect Barney on my way up onto the moors, but she was never in evidence. I knew from Rosie's chatter and occasional comments from Tom that she was around, keeping a low profile, and never going anywhere near the baby if she could help it.

Then one morning I let myself into the kitchen at Black Combe and there she was, just her, seated at the kitchen table. She had a mug of coffee in front of her and looked to have just got up. Her feet were bare, her hair still tangled from bed. I recognized the shirt she was wearing as one of Nathan's, her long, bare legs crossed under the table. And there was no sign of Barney.

She looked up, seemed unsurprised to see me waltzing into her kitchen. "Morning. Coffee?" She smiled at me, jerked her head in the direction of the coffee pot. "I just brewed some, thought you might be turning up sometime soon."

So she was apparently expecting me then. And seemed inclined to be sociable. Intimidated or not, I don't have enough friends to turn down an opportunity so I nodded, muttered my thanks, and went to help myself.

Sitting opposite Eva in the kitchen at Black Combe, I found I had absolutely nothing to say to her. What does a convicted liar and self-confessed thief find to say to an accomplished academic, a respected musician? And Eva seemed to be in no rush to make small talk, having apparently done her social duty by making the coffee. At a bit of a loss I decided to fall back on the sole topic of conversation I could come up with.

"So, I understand you've been ill. How are you feeling now?"

She looked at me, her face giving nothing much away. Then, "Ill? Is that what you call it? Not suicidal? Mentally unstable? A crap mother?"

I regarded her, long and hard. If she wanted to pick a fight, why bother making me coffee? And I decided not to rise to it. I may not have her brains, but I'm definitely not stupid. Falling out with Nathan's beloved Eva would not be a good move, not for me, not for any of us. I decided to make an effort.

"No, I call it ill. And the fact that you're down here rather than huddled up in bed suggests to me you're getting better, and I'm glad about that. And I was here that day, when you first got back. I know what happened, and I know it was an accident."

She shakes her head, her lips quirked in a wry, self-effacing smile. "An accident waiting to happen."

I shrug. "Whatever, but they all count." And I decided that was enough socializing for one day. "Thanks for the coffee. Is Barney anywhere about?"

"He's upstairs. In the shower." She smiles at my astonished expression. "It seems he went out and rolled in something particularly vile and Grace refused to let him back in the house until he'd been swilled down. She dragged him off upstairs. It's gonna take a whole crate of Head and Shoulders to wash that bloody dog..."

I can't imagine shampooing Barney is easy. "Can Grace manage, do you think?" Any excuse to get out of there.

No help to be had from Eva, it seems. "I expect so. My mum's up there too. I think they've got it covered. They left me in charge down here. All part of the great plan to make me feel useful. It's not working."

At my puzzled look, she jerked her head in the direction of the corner behind me. I turned, to see baby Isabella tucked up nice and secure in her baby seat, fast asleep. I smiled, couldn't help it. She's so sweet. I turned back to Eva, resolved to maybe stay a little bit longer. "Can I pick her up? I'll try not to wake her. Please."

She waved expansively in the direction of the baby. "Be my guest. She's due a feed any time now in any case. Tell you what, I'll make the bottle, and you give it to her."

And so, that's how we came that morning to be sitting companionably in the kitchen at Black Combe, me feeding a very appreciative Isabella her bottle while Eva quizzed me about Tom.

"So, you and Tom then? I'm glad he's found someone. He's a lovely man, always kind to me."

I nodded. I think Tom's probably kind to everyone. Hell, he was even kind to me, eventually. These days he's especially personable when he has a whip in his hand, but I didn't see any reason to dwell on that. But Eva was on a quest, wanted more. "So how did you and Tom meet then?"

Ah, now that *was* the six million dollar question. And quite suddenly, there and then, and bearing in mind I'd never clapped eyes on this woman before in my life, I told her. The full story, about that awful night in Bristol and about me turning up here quite by chance. I didn't tell her about Tom's reaction when he first saw me, when he recognized me and decided I needed to be taught some sort of a lesson—I think maybe that's a tale for another day. Eva listened to me, never commented, never turned a hair. Her only response was to observe what a small world it is, and I found myself compelled to agree.

We fell silent for a while, both of us I'm sure wondering if, how, to broach the issue uppermost in our minds. I know that Nathan's a Dom too, and from what Tom told me I'm pretty sure Eva's his sub. But it's not exactly the sort of thing you can come right out and ask. Or is it? Eva seemed to think it was worth a try. She may have been somewhat taciturn when I'd first arrived in her kitchen, but she was positively garrulous now and certainly prepared to have a go.

"Yes, Tom's a nice guy. Very good looking too, in a sort of Adonis way."

"Adonis?"

"Mmm, Greek god of beauty and desire."

"Ah, right." *Yes, definitely sounds about right to me.*

"And sort of — masterful. Dominating. Don't you think so?"

She cocked her head to one side, looked at me expectantly. I returned her gaze, steady, serious — before I lost it and collapsed into laughter. Even Isabella was moved to complain as the flow of her milk was rudely interrupted by my helpless giggling. Eva joined in, and it was clear we had a perfect understanding.

At last, able to speak again, I responded politely, "Yes, very Dominant. I have on occasions had the scars to prove it, though they don't usually last very long."

Eva just nodded wisely, she is after all my senior by nearly two years. "I find arnica helpful. Probably best to buy in some extra, just give me a shout if you want some."

I thanked her politely. We both smiled and reached an understanding.

So now, Eva and I are firm friends. She's always around as I collect Barney, we often share a morning coffee together. And occasionally she comes out with me, Rosie and Barney, up onto the moors. Never too far, or for too long. She's not well still, gets tired easily. But I enjoy her company, and oddly enough she seems to like mine. We laugh a lot, mostly about Tom and Nathan. I'm not sure if subs are supposed to discuss their Doms and compare notes. Neither is Eva, but we do it. All the time. She's been back about six seeks now, and is clearly staying. Rosie's over the moon, Nathan's a different man too. And I just love having a friend.

Chapter Two

"Are you out and about today?" Tom glances at me across the breakfast table, his marmalade toast dangling from his fingers. I smile, remembering just where those sticky fingers were half an hour ago. I do enjoy mornings at Greystones, and surely there can be no more civilized way to greet the day than with a mind-blowing orgasm. Still, back to the business in hand.

"Yes, later probably. Depends a bit on the light quality. I'm after getting some nice smudgy horizon shots, so a bit of heat haze would be useful. What's the weather forecast, do you know?"

He shoves the last of his toast in his mouth and chews it before answering, "Of course I know. I'm a bloody farmer, it's my job to know. You should be all right—dry, sunny, temperatures reaching twenty-two centigrade. Will that do you?"

I nod then go to put more bread in the toaster. I'm quite proud of my prowess with toast these days, it's really very simple when you know how.

"I shot a fox earlier. Saw it sniffing around the outside of the poultry run first thing. I definitely hit it because there was blood on the wall where it scrambled over, but the crafty little bugger got away. I don't like leaving a job unfinished, so if you happen to spot it could you text me and let me know where it is?"

I turn to him, and I confess I'm a little shocked at his callous attitude. I know foxes are pests, but still… He sees my expression and stands up, comes to give me a hug.

"Don't go getting all sentimental, love. You'd soon lose your fondness for foxes if you saw the state of a poultry shed after one had been visiting. Blood and carnage everywhere. They're a menace around farms."

I shake my head. "But even so, can't you…? I mean, you're supposed to be humane aren't you?"

"Indeed I am. And I'm also a farmer with a living to make. I'd prefer to have killed it cleanly, though, so if you do spot it anywhere let me know and I'll finish the job. Okay?"

I shrug and mumble something along the lines of, "If I have to…"

Tom just chuckles, that lovely, sexy laugh of his. "You live on a farm now, Miss McAllister. Get with the program."

* * * *

It's late afternoon and I'm making my way back down from an area known locally as Black Moor, high above Haworth. I've managed to get some decent images, including the lovely smudgy horizons I was looking for, so life's good as I trundle across the springy moorland grass on my quad. Barney is ambling alongside, his quiet company always welcome. Eva was having an off day so didn't want to come with me, and Rosie's at some after school club I gather so it's just me and my big furry friend.

I've traveled a few yards farther before I realize Barney has stopped, standing stock still, his ears cocked. I stop and wait for him. He doesn't move so I twist round in the seat and try calling him. I could do with getting back home before too much longer—I have images to upload onto my computer, work to do.

Barney's having none of it. He turns away from me, starts to inch across the grassy slope toward a patch of dark brown bracken. He's crouching, his ears back as though he's stalking something. As I watch him, wondering what on earth he thinks is in there, he comes to a stop and starts barking at whatever he thinks is hidden in the undergrowth.

Curious, I switch off the engine, and it's only then that I hear what Barney's sharper ears must have picked out. A high-pitched squealing sound, a sound made by something quite small in a lot of distress. We do occasionally get poachers around here, setting cruel traps for rabbits. I'm pretty sure what I'm hearing isn't a rabbit—as far as I know they don't make any sound—but maybe something else has got trapped. I make my way cautiously over to Barney, leaning over him to look at whatever he's found.

It's a fox. Tom's fox I don't doubt. Sure enough, I can see its right hind leg has a nasty gunshot wound, although the blood looks to be dried up pretty much. Still, the animal is in a bad way. It's not dead, not quite. I can see its flanks moving as it breathes, but its eyes are closed and it seems unaware of our presence. It's definitely not the fox making all that din.

But first things first. I pull out my phone and shoot a quick text off to Tom.

Found your fox. Still alive – just. On edge of Black Moor, about 100 yds west of footpath. Do you want me to wait till you get here?

His reply isn't long in coming –

Would you? That'll help me to find it. See you in 10.

He must have got held up as it's closer to fifteen minutes before I spot Tom's Land Rover bouncing over the rough moorland, about a mile below me. I wave at him, both arms above my head, and see the moment he spots me and turns in my direction. A few minutes later he's jumping from the Land Rover, his shotgun broken across his elbow.

He drops a kiss on my forehead. "I knew I could rely on you, sweetheart. Where is it then?"

I point to Barney, still standing guard. I can't take the credit either.

"Barney found it, not me."

"What a team." He tosses the words back as he strides away from me, and is soon crouching alongside Barney, examining the state of the poor fox. He stands, turns back to me.

"Would you mind getting Barney out of the way – don't want any accidents?"

I nod and reach for Barney's huge collar. I doubt there's going to be much I can do about it if the mountain of a dog decides he wants to stand his ground, but luckily he's in a cooperative mood and lets me tug him out of the immediate vicinity. I turn my back, knowing what's coming, but still I flinch as I hear the shot.

"Right. That's one sorted, now where's the other?" Tom has started pacing around, looking at the ground, moving in circles around the carcass of the fox.

"Other? What other?"

"The cub. That's what's making all that noise. You must have heard it?"

A fox cub! I never even considered that possibility. The dead fox must have been a mother with a young cub, and now the baby's somewhere nearby screaming its head off. I scurry to catch up with Tom and join in the search.

Barney soon comes up trumps again though, and in a few minutes is standing with his nose in the bracken, sniffing at something on the ground. We both crouch next to him and sure enough there it is. A cute and fluffy little red fox cub. It's squealing loudly — frantic, high-pitched squeaks that tell of hunger and fear and loneliness. My heart turns over as I reach out to stroke it.

Tom catches my wrist before I can touch the little furry creature.

"Careful, it's a wild animal even if it does look like a puppy dog. And it'll be riddled with fleas. You get Barney out of the way, I'll see to this."

He starts to re-load his shotgun, and I realize he means to shoot this poor little orphan. I grab his arm, determined that's not going to happen. How could he? How could anyone?

"You can't do that. The poor little thing's hungry, and cold, and…"

"It's vermin. In another few months it'll be helping itself to my chickens. Or it would have been." He closes the gun and stands, the barrel pointing down.

Instinctively I position myself between Tom and the cub. Tom gives me a narrow, withering look and breaks the gun open again for safety.

He tries to convince me. "Look, love, it won't survive on its own anyway. It's too young to fend for itself. Kinder for me to put it out of its misery now rather than let it starve to death."

I'm not having that. This is a baby, for Christ's sake. He can't just kill a baby. I can hear the pleading note in my voice as I try to reason with him. "We could look after it, rear it until it's old enough to set free."

Tom looks at me as though I've just been beamed in from Mars. The idea, the very notion of hand-rearing a fox cub then letting it go is as alien to him as my old life in Bristol now seems to me.

"Like hell we will. There's no way I'm taking that thing back to my farm, wasting good food on it, just to let it go so's it can help itself to my fucking chickens. Christ, they even take piglets if they can get past the sows." His tone is exasperated, his expression one of utter incredulity.

I can see he'll never relent.

And neither will I. There's no way I'm letting this happen. I unzip my light hoodie and slip it off.

"Now what are you doing?" He sounds pretty pissed off, I don't get the impression he thinks I'm stripping for his benefit. He's right.

"I'm taking it home. I'll look after it."

"You're not taking it home, Ashley. Not happening. No way is that bloody fox going anywhere near Greystones."

I'm just as angry as Tom now, and I give up any attempt to plead with him. I turn and reach for the still squealing little cub and wrap it in my hoodie. I stand to face him again, this time cradling the noisy bundle in my arms.

"Not Greystones. *My* home. My cottage. Get out of my way." I make to shove past him, but Tom grips my elbow. He makes one last attempt to assert his authority in this matter.

"Ashley, last chance now. Put the cub down, get back on your quad and go to the farm. I'll finish off here and see you at home. Do it now." His voice is stern, unrelenting, all Dom. It shakes me a little, I've never seen this facet of Tom outside of a scening situation and I know he expects me to obey him. Normally I would, without question, but every fiber of my being insists I protect this helpless fox cub.

I don't drop my gaze and naturally neither does Tom. He waits for me to back down and obey him. I can't, not in this. At last I just shake my head and step around him. He makes no further attempt to stop me, and I manage to scramble onto my quad and start the engine, my precious little bundle huddled in my lap.

I glance back up the hillside when I reach the wider bridle path at the bottom. Tom's Land Rover is still there and I see him sling something onto the back of it—no doubt the dead vixen. And even my loyal companion Barney seems to have opted to stay with Tom.

Tom turns in my direction as I make my way along the bridle path, and seems to be watching me ride away from him. My temper, always a short-lived fizzle at best, has cooled on the way down, and now my heart is sinking as I ask myself how something so simple ever came to this? How could a sweet little orphaned fox cub cause such a rift? Tom doesn't issue many instructions, but when he does, he means them. And deep down I do know he's right about the practical realities of foxes around his livestock. But I couldn't just let him kill the cub. Could I?

When I arrive back at Smithy's Forge about half an hour later, the place is cold and unwelcoming. I haven't spent a night here in months, but I still carry the key on my key ring so I let myself in, the tiny fox cub still bundled in my hoodie. Even though I call in every few days to pick up my post and just check the place over, there's no food in—for me or the cub. No hot water and only a couple of logs beside the stove to heat the place. Luckily it's summer so the cottage isn't cold, but I still don't see how I'll be able to manage. Most of my clothes are at Tom's, as is all my equipment for doing my work. I really have not thought this through at all.

I pull out a drawer from my small kitchen dresser to dump the cub in for the time being, Maybe if I nip down into the village I can pick up some milk. *I wonder if foxes like cow's milk?* Or I could call at Tom's vending machine, which is closer. On second thoughts, that's probably rubbing salt in.

The squealing is now reaching fever pitch and I know I have to do something. But what? Despite my determination to be some sort of foster mum, I really haven't the first idea of how to care for a fox cub. I sink into my fireside chair, with no idea at all what the hell to do next.

My phone tinkles, a text has arrived. I tap the screen to open the message. Naturally, it's from Tom.

Phoned RSPCA in Bradford. They'll take the cub. Will that do?

I hit reply, and type in my response.

Thank you. I should have thought of that. I'll take the cub there. Whereabouts in Bradford?

His reply is quick in coming and curt.

I'll send you a link to their website. It has directions and a map. Then I want you to come straight back here to the farm. Is that clear?

He seems very, very angry still. Angry Doms are difficult to be around I've found. I don't expect my homecoming to be a joyful affair. But first, the cub...

* * * *

An hour and a half later, I'm turning into the Greystones driveway, my little squeaking charge safely deposited with the kind people down at the RSPCA. They promised me they'd take care of it, rear it until it's big enough to fend for itself, then they'll set it free somewhere. I just hope it's somewhere a long way from Greystones.

I pull up next to the vending machine then get out of the car to close the gate behind me. Some aspects of farming life have become ingrained it seems, and I strongly suspect I'm about to learn a few more hard lessons in the very near future. My bottom clenches, and I'm surprised to note this is not in an entirely bad way, as I consider what is without doubt in store for me at the farmhouse.

I pull up around the back next to the Land Rover and climb out. I lock my car before making my way to the kitchen door. I'm almost as nervous as I was that first morning when I came here to clean, to start my atonement for the attack on Tom two years previously. The door is unlocked as usual, and I slip inside. The kitchen is empty apart from my young cats who are snoozing in their box beside the Aga. They ignore me as I wander from room to room looking for Tom. I'm dreading finding him, but at the same time it feels so lonely here without him. The farm is empty, quiet and cool, not at all to my liking. I know the temperature is no different from usual probably, but it still feels chilly to me.

My phone tinkles again, and I drag it from my pocket. The text gives me my instructions.

Go to bedroom and choose a belt from my wardrobe. Then come to barn. DON'T keep me waiting.

Well, now I know. Less than two minutes later I'm hurrying across the yard toward the barn, a stout belt from Tom's extensive collection looped around my arm. The door is standing open so I go straight inside.

I have to wait a few moments to let my eyes adjust to the dim light but soon pick out Tom down at the far end of the huge space. He's leaning against a stack of hay bales, facing me. His arms are folded across his chest, his ankles crossed. He looks terrifying, stern, angry and about to deliver retribution. All this for a tiny little defenseless fox cub.

I make my way toward him, wondering if perhaps even now I can talk my way out of this. After all, just disagreeing with Tom, even about something to do with his farm, is hardly a capital offense. I soon dismiss that notion. I might as well have tried to remove my own appendix with a knife and fork. It's a total non-starter. He doesn't even let me get a word in.

"Hand me the belt. Drop your jeans and your underwear, and bend over this bale."

I hesitate, really scared suddenly. He's only once before laid a hand on me in genuine retribution and that *was* only his hand. Not a thick, heavy belt. This is going to hurt. A lot.

"Please, Tom, I'm sorry..."

"Do as I say. Now. When you're bending over the bale, your bottom bare and ready for me, then you can start telling me what you're sorry for." His Dom voice cuts off my attempt to apologize, echoing around the barn. He doesn't shout at me, he never does, but that icy tone grabs me every time.

I start to unfasten my jeans, my hands shaking.

"The boots too. I want you naked from the waist down."

"What if someone comes in? Seth or maybe one of his sons?"

He smiles, but there's no warmth there. "You'll just have to hope they don't. You could always try not to make too much noise — the sound of you screaming might attract more attention than you really want. I don't mind an audience for this, but you may feel differently."

I certainly do. I kick off my boots then finish removing my jeans and underwear before moving to stand in front of the bale he's decided to use. I notice that he's spread a blanket over it, which I suppose is fairly considerate in the circumstances.

"Is the cub sorted out now then?"

I nod, and thank him again for suggesting the RSPCA.

He flexes the belt in his hands, now eying my bare bottom with interest. I clench my buttocks, at the same time curling my toes in the dry straw beneath my feet. Punishment or not, he's certainly managing to release my inner submissive this time.

"I could see how strongly you felt about the cub. I may be hard-headed about some aspects of farming, but I was always going to find a compromise. For you. You should have trusted me."

His reply surprises me, but he's right. I should have. I should have stayed, talked to him. He'd never have shot the cub without my agreement. Apart from anything else, he'd have had to move me out of the way. Tom may be handy with a whip or a strap, but he's never rough, never manhandles me. He wouldn't have moved me by force. Suddenly contrite, I apologize again and this time I do really mean it— "You're right, and I'm sorry. And I can see you're right about foxes too. I should have listened to you."

He nods briefly. "Yes, Ashley. You should. You don't have to agree, but you should at least listen. I *did* listen to you and found another way to deal with the problem. But you're new to farm life, and you've a lot to learn. It'll come. That's not why we're here though."

Isn't it? I look up at him, surprised.

"We're here because you walked out on me." He pauses, lets that sink in before he elaborates further. "We argued, disagreed about something, and you pissed off. Went back to 'your home' as you called it. *This* is your home, Ashley, and I don't want you to forget that again. And that's why I'm teaching you this lesson. Commitment means you don't just bail out of our relationship at the first sign of trouble. You stay, we work on it. We talk. I wouldn't have walked out on you, I won't, whatever happens. I expect the same commitment from you. Do I have it?"

I stare at him, horrified. And deeply ashamed. It's true. I did do exactly that. I wanted my own way, so I just stopped listening to Tom, ignored his point of view. Instead I leaped onto my quad and left him there on the moor. I deserve the beating he's about to administer. If I could, I'd do it myself.

I step forward and lean across the hay bale, settling my upper body on the blanket.

"I'm ready."

"Yes, you are. Or very nearly. One last thing though, Ashley." He leans on the bale alongside me, his hip propped against the hay.

I turn, peer at him over my shoulder. Maybe he intends to tie me up first.

Apparently not. It seems he has more to say. "This is the second time I've punished you when you've done something that pissed me off. The first time, that first day when I came to your cottage, you hated it. Hated me probably."

I shake my head, start to deny it.

He silences me with one raised finger. "Quiet please, and listen. Okay, so you may not have hated me, but you hated being spanked, even if I did give you an orgasm afterwards. And you were certainly terrified then, and in the days after. You're behaving very differently now. Why is that?"

I gaze up at him, and I find I'm wondering the same thing. Why *is* this different? Before I can scrape together any sort of response, he reaches out and lightly caresses my bottom. The bottom he's soon intending to thrash with his belt. I remain still, my toes curling and my pussy moistening as he continues to massage my buttocks, increasing the pressure until I'm squirming with arousal.

"I know Kenny used to hit you, when he was angry. Maybe even when he wasn't. Did you lie still and allow him to stroke your bum first like this, or maybe finger fuck you, like this?" His voice is soft, a sexy, sensual murmur as he leans over me, his wonderful, talented fingers working smoothly to bring me to a glittering orgasm.

I gasp, and my head falls forward to rest on the blanket as he slides his fingers between my legs and sinks three of them deep into my pussy. I spread my thighs without him needing to ask, and he moves now to stand immediately behind me. He's laid the belt on top of the bale, and is using his free hand to reach between my legs to rub my clit.

It doesn't take long. It never does when Tom decides I'm to come, and come fast. He thrusts his fingers deep, angling to hit my sensitive G-spot, and lightly squeezes my clit. He grips the throbbing nub between his index and middle finger and flicks the tip with the pad of his thumb. It's too much, and in moments I'm moaning as my climax builds and erupts, all my nerve endings seemingly connected to that little button under his thumb. I grasp the blanket, curling my fingers in it as I rotate my hips, silently begging him to fuck me. He doesn't do that though, not yet. Instead he continues to slide his fingers in and out of my pussy as I clench and spasm around him, squeezing hard to generate more friction, more sensation.

"Greedy little slut. That's enough for now I think. More later. When you've learnt your lesson and I'm sure it's sunk in." He withdraws his fingers, and I lie there, gasping. His tone has hardened, and I know this interlude is over. On to the main event, the main reason we're here and I'm draped half naked across a bale of hay.

He leans over me, his hands on either side of my shoulders, his face close to my ear. "Is this different from Kenny?"

Christ, yes!

"How, Ashley? How is it different?"

I didn't realize I spoke out loud, but I suppose I must have. And now he's insisting on an answer.

"How, Ashley? Think, and tell me."

"Because it's you. You won't hurt me."

"I think you know I will."

"No, not really. And you'll stop if I ask you to. If I say my safe word."

"So, you know it's going to hurt. But you'll still allow me to punish you. Is this abuse then, Ashley, or something else?"

I'm trying hard to concentrate, but in my post-orgasmic haze, it's difficult to think straight. One thing I am sure of though, there's nothing in the least bit abusive about Tom Shore. He loves me, I love him and this is how we resolve our differences. No sulking, no harsh words or cruelty. We have rules, and he enforces those rules. Then it's over, and we're even more closely connected than we were before.

"Ashley? Do you feel I'm abusing you? Bullying you? I want you to say so if you do."

I shake my head vehemently, partly in denial and partly to clear my thinking. My voice is a whisper, but that has nothing to do with fear now. This is a deeply emotional moment, a pivotal point in our relationship. I know better than to move before he tells me I can, but I'm yearning just to turn to face him and sink my fingers into his hair as he sinks his cock into me. Nothing less will do now, but first we have unfinished business.

"No, I don't feel that. I love you, and I know you love me. I deserve to be punished. Please do it."

He straightens. "Happy to oblige, my sweet. I think twenty strokes would be about right. Would you agree?"

I nod contentedly and flex my fingers in the blanket. "Yes, twenty sounds perfect."

He reaches across me to pick up the belt then takes his position behind me, slightly to my left.

"This is going to be just a little bit too hard for you to really enjoy it. It is a punishment after all. But do your best. I'd like you to count the strokes please. Are you ready?"

I nod, and a moment later the first stroke lands, sharp and searing across my right buttock. I yelp in pain, but manage not to move. And I even remember to count.

"One. Thank you. More please."

The next stroke lands on my left buttock. I whimper again, but my voice is firm as I count. "Two. Thank you. The next one, please."

By the time we reach ten my bottom feels to be on fire, a familiar sensation these days and one I know I can usually cope with. Enjoy even. Tom wasn't bluffing though when he promised to make this beating a hard one, and I'm conscious of only being at the half way mark. The next ten will be a struggle.

"Are you okay to continue?" Tom has laid the belt down on the straw and is leaning over me again. "Open your eyes, Ashley. Let me know you're all right."

It's an effort, but I manage to prize my eyelids open. I even manage a small but probably far from convincing smile for him. It's enough though.

"Ten more, then we're done. I want you to continue counting and I'll wait for you to say the number before each stroke. Ready to carry on?"

My slight nod is enough and the eleventh stroke lands on the back of my right thigh. That's a sensitive spot for me, so this really hurts, and I know I won't be sitting comfortably for at least two days. Maybe more.

"Eleven. Christ, Tom..."

"Just count, or you can thank me if you want to. Nothing else."

The next strike lands on my left thigh, and I gasp the number. "Twelve." I can't bring myself to ask for more, or to thank him for his efforts.

He chuckles, well aware that I'm struggling now, his punishment is having the desired effect. I know he's watching me carefully though, and whether I safe word or not, he'll stop if he has to. I absolutely trust him to do that, so I relax into the blanket, my eyes closed and my teeth gritted, and I ready myself for the next blow. And the next, and the next.

We've reached fifteen, and I'm regretting not asking him to tie me to the bale. It's a real struggle to remain on my feet. Tom peels back the edge of the blanket to reveal the hay beneath and helps me to curl my fingers around the rope stretched tightly around the whole thing, holding it all together.

"Hang on to that. And don't stop counting."

A few seconds go by then number sixteen lands across my upper left thigh, right at the crease where it joins the lower curve of my bottom. I know my buttocks and the backs of my legs must be covered in deep red stripes, and without doubt this lesson is one I will never forget. I manage to whisper the number, and tighten my vice-like grip on the rope to stop myself from sliding off the bale. Just four more. That's not much, surely I can manage that.

I might think so, but Tom has other ideas.

"Enough. We're done here." He drops the belt onto the floor and reaches for me. He turns me carefully, wrapping the blanket around me before he lifts me in his arms and strides out of the barn. I'm not sure whether to be relieved or disappointed. I really thought I could complete the twenty, but I hurt like crazy now, everywhere, and I'm glad Tom called a halt.

He carries me inside and straight upstairs, placing me face down on our bed.

"You need a long soak. Then a slow and very thorough fucking. Sound good to you?"

I sigh. "Yes, that sounds wonderful." Every muscle is aching, my body feels to be on fire, I hurt in places I never even knew I had, but I feel utterly contented. Cared for. Loved.

And there's no doubt at all in my mind regarding where my home is.

Chapter Three

I opt to stay at home for the next few days, my body still stiff from my encounter in the barn. Eva wonders why I'm not collecting Barney and uses that as an excuse to take a walk over the moors to Greystones to find out what has happened to me. She only has to look at me and she knows the score.

"Show me."

"No!"

"Yes. Skirt up, knickers down."

"Christ, you sound like Tom. And I'm not wearing any knickers."

"Ah. I see. Bad as that? Well show me then. Now."

I sigh, knowing she won't let up any time soon. I turn around, raising my skirt to let her see the damage. She's not especially impressed by my battle scars.

"Mmm, hardly a mark on you. You should see my arse sometimes. I reckon Tom's just a big softie. So, how long are you going to lounge around here for? We want you two to come over to dinner sometime soon. What about next week? That'll give me time to come up with something I can actually manage to cook."

A truly immovable force, Eva Byrne. Again I surrender to the inevitable. "All right. I'll check with Tom and let you know. As far as I can remember though we've not got any pressing engagements coming up."

* * * *

Eva's not long left and I'm trying to concentrate on the noble art of digital painting. I start with a basic image, in this case a winter landscape, then overlay that with other images to build a new and uniquely intriguing picture. My tastes tend toward the fantastic these days, so I'm creating a lunar landscape. I've dropped a couple of extinct volcanoes in, and I'm just contemplating how best to create a meteor storm when my phone rings.

Tom probably. He should have been back about half an hour ago but must have gotten held up somewhere. I reach for my phone, ever-present alongside my laptop and tap the green icon to take the call.

It's not Tom. It's Seth Appleyard.

"Ashley? Miss McAllister?" Always polite, almost to a fault, is our Mr Appleyard.

"Seth, hello. How are you?"

"I'm fine, Miss, thanks for asking. But it's Tom. Mr Shore. He's had an accident."

My heart plummets and I almost drop my phone, my fingers suddenly nerveless. *Tom? An accident? Oh, Christ! Oh no.* My head is instantly filled with gory images, blood, guts and severed limbs. I know how dangerous farming can be even in a well-run place like Greystones.

"What? What's happened? Where is he?" I'm stammering, my voice already starting to break.

"He's on his way to hospital. Air ambulance. He asked me to let you know."

Thank God for that, at least he was conscious then. At some stage. But, Christ, the air ambulance?

I'm already digging in my pockets for my car keys as I quiz Seth. "But, what happened? How bad is he?"

The main news imparted, Seth is a man of few words now. "Tractor overturned. Mr Shore was trapped underneath it, but we managed to get him out. He was talking, but crush injuries can be nasty. The ambulance crew wanted him in hospital."

Crush injuries. Christ!

"Which hospital? Airedale?"

"Yes. Do you want me to come and pick you up, take you down there?"

By now I'm already half way out of the door, my car keys in my hand. "No. No thanks, I'll make my own way. I know where it is." My voice is shaking, but every instinct now is screaming at me to get to where Tom is.

"Okay. I'll see you there then. Bye, Miss McAllister."

I hang up, forgetting to say goodbye. Moments later I'm hurtling down the narrow lane heading for Keighley, Airedale General and Tom.

* * * *

Crush injuries can indeed be nasty, but mercifully Tom is not after all to be the proof of that. His injuries amount to a monster concussion and a few badly bruised ribs. The hospital want to keep him in overnight for observation, but as long as no other complications surface he should be home tomorrow.

Sitting beside Tom in a quiet side ward, I can't help crying with relief. Reassured, Seth has departed to take care of things back at Greystones. I'm clutching Tom's hand and trying not to look too closely at the electronic gadgetry arranged around him. All of it is merely precautionary, the nurse has assured me, but still it terrifies me.

The last time I was in a hospital, my baby was dead, and I know I came perilously close to losing Tom today. My stomach lurches, I actually feel faint just contemplating that. Over the last couple of years I've got used to loss, or I should have. I've had plenty of practice. I now realize I'm nowhere near immune to grief and pain, and Tom is as vital to me as oxygen. I grasp his hand tighter, determined never to let go.

"Sweetheart, don't cry. It's nowhere near as bad as it looks. Hurts when I laugh though…"

His wry smile just makes me more weepy. Resigned, he leaves me to cry for a while, get it out of my system. Tom has never encouraged me to bottle up my feelings, so he settles for stroking my hair as I lay my head on his pristine white hospital covers and sob.

Eventually my sobs give way to a bout of unladylike gulping and hiccupping. He laughs at me, and I see what he means about his ribs hurting as he winces and grunts in pain. Serves him right for scaring me like that, and now that the initial shock has subsided I can find it in me to be unsympathetic.

He retaliates. "So, I guess all this outpouring of grief means I'm forgiven for the other day, when I threatened to murder your fox cub, and then took my belt to you."

I glance around, hoping none of the hospital staff are within earshot. His remarks might take some explaining. I punch his arm.

"Idiot. Keep your voice down."

He shakes his head sadly, his expression grave. "Oh, dear, I suspect our next serious conversation will have to be about respect. And not calling your Dom an idiot, especially when he's laid up with cracked ribs."

I see his smile, hovering at the corners of his lips, and the familiar twinkle in those gorgeous green eyes, and decide to push my luck.

"Cracked now? They were only bruised a few minutes ago."

"Have a care, Miss McAllister. Your lovely bottom hasn't entirely recovered from our last visit to the barn."

"You and whose army, Mr Shore? You don't look to me as though you could lift a pencil, let alone a spanking paddle."

"Well maybe I'll have to help him out then. After all, what are friends for?"

I whirl in my seat to see Nathan lounging in the doorway, grinning at us. Well, at me mainly. He continues, obviously enjoying himself immensely, "Is that right, Tom? You need an army to help you sort out your cheeky little sub?"

Tom shifts in the bed, winking at me before assuring Nathan that whilst it might be a struggle, he's sure he'll eventually rise to the occasion. I flush beetroot. My face burns, right to the roots of my hair. Mortified, I try to collect my wits as Nathan pulls a plastic chair from a stack in the corridor outside Tom's side ward and makes himself comfortable next to me. He peers critically at Tom for a few moments, appraising the damage, then launches in with his questions, "Well, you don't look as bad as I expected. What have they said?"

Tom shrugs, and from his grimace I get the impression that's painful too. "Just bruises and concussion. Could have been worse."

Privately I'm also in total agreement, but I offer no further comment.

Nathan nods. "So, how long are you going to be stuck in here?"

"Till tomorrow probably. Then they say I can come home as long as I take things easy." His expression leaves the pair of us in no doubt regarding his opinion of that prospect, and now it's Nathan's turn to be unsympathetic. He has it down to a fine art.

"Bed rest, that's what you need. And chicken soup. I'll have a word with Grace."

"Fuck off if that's the best you can come up with. Me and Ashley were talking."

"Ah, right. You were just discussing your current predicament. Is she in need of a spanking then? My offer still stands."

I flinch and might have squeaked. They both turn to me, grinning broadly, and Tom takes my hand

"She'll keep. And stop embarrassing my sub, if you don't mind. She's had a bad day."

Nathan looks at me more closely, obviously concerned now. "Yes, I can see that. Sorry, love, didn't mean to upset you. When you've done fussing over the wounded soldier here, we want you to come over to Black Combe. Grace'll have the spare room ready. Eva reckons you shouldn't be rattling around that farmhouse on your own, and I think she's probably right. She usually is. Comes of having a PhD I suppose."

I have no doubt regarding the strength of Eva's credentials, but I shake my head, not wanting to put them out.

Nathan's having none of it. "You'll come, or I'll send Grace to fetch you. You really don't want to be arguing with Grace."

And so it's settled.

The matter of my accommodation for the night resolved, and my initial shock now quite dissipated, I'm sufficiently calm to be able to ask Tom what on earth happened. Nathan also seems to want the gory details and leans forward on his elbows to hear the explanation. I presume Tom's been driving tractors for years without mishap, so what went wrong today? His answer is succinct.

"Moles."

"What?" I'm not sure I heard right. Nathan neither apparently, as he glances to me for some sort of translation. We both return our gaze to the patient, at a loss.

"Fucking moles."

Ah. That's what I thought he said. I try to formulate some sort of coherent image. Swerving the tractor to miss a jaywalking mole? Distracted by some X-rated moley antics somewhere close by? What? How?

"You mean moles, fucking?" Nathan helpfully seeks to clarify, obviously on the same wavelength as me. Who'd have imagined that?

Tom chuckles, no doubt at the expression of absolute mystification plastered across both our face. And he decides to elaborate.

"Fucking moles, digging their tunnels under my lower meadow. They make the ground spongy, and if there's too much underground activity it creates caverns. A heavy tractor can easily overturn. Mine did."

Nathan's just as bemused as me. "But, can't you see where they've been? I mean, you rustic types can tell things like that by sniffing the air can't you? Wouldn't there be molehills or something? Some clue?"

I might have been a little more polite, but essentially my questions would have been much the same. Tom looks at him patiently, obviously used to Nathan's general ignorance of rural affairs.

"Not necessarily. And there aren't always molehills. If I'd known the little bastards had been scurrying about under there I wouldn't have driven a fucking fifty grand tractor across it, would I? Which reminds me, I need to sort out the insurance. Hope it covers moles."

Me too. A fifty grand tractor disappearing under a meadow sounds like a big deal. I wonder if moles qualify as an act of God? And I also wonder how we'll get rid of the things now they've taken up residence under Tom's fields. My nerves won't stand another day like this.

"What can we do about them?" I blurt out the question, and both men turn to me.

Tom seems to think the matter of marauding moles is under control. "Seth will already have all that in hand. We have a few remedies of our own we can try, and if all else fails we'll call in the professionals. Mole-Busters. Unless you have anything particular in mind, Ashley?" Tom looks genuinely interested, but then ruins it. "After all, I know your views on protecting wildlife."

"Ah, yes, the fox cub. I heard about that." Nathan looks amused and I know I have Eva to thank. *Is nothing to be considered private around here?*

Tom takes pity on me. "We'll recover the tractor, and hopefully the insurance will cough up and it'll be fixed. Then we stay off that field until the moles are no longer in residence and the ground settles again. Unless you fancy spending a few nights up there with a shotgun. You could blast the buggers every time one pops its head up. We could even start a mole-whacking visitor attraction, like at a fair, and make some money out of it. How does that sound?"

It sounds fucking stupid to me, and I tell him so. Before I punch him again, and he finally orders Nathan to take me home so I can't do him any further damage.

Chapter Four

Dinner at Black Combe the following week is actually a wonderful evening. Tom's now pretty much fully recovered, and the terrifying incident of the tractor and the moles has been relegated to a matter for joking about. I could never have imagined this just a few months ago, the four of us just laughing and enjoying each other's company, the proceedings helped along nicely by Nathan's twenty quid a bottle red wine of course. Tom made good on his promise regarding a lesson in respect, and once more I'm not able to sit comfortably. Eva keeps grinning each time I shift in my chair. Tom can't quite conceal his smirk either. It's a knocking bet that someone has let Nathan in on the secret too, though just for this evening he's on his best behavior and apparently too polite to let anything slip.

We knock back quite a lot of Nathan's fine wine between us, so Tom and I stay over.

* * * *

Both the men have early starts, well early-ish, so it's just me, Eva and Grace enjoying a late breakfast around the Black Combe kitchen table at around eleven the following morning. I'm once again giving Isabella her bottle, having begged Grace and Eva to let me do the honors.

"So, will you have any more children, do you think?" Eva eyes me across the toast and marmalade, her question quiet but intuitive.

Grace excuses herself, something about having washing to sort out upstairs

I shake my head, emphatic, vehement. "No, not me. Once is enough. I couldn't go through all that again."

I had related the story of my ill-fated pregnancy early on in our acquaintance. Eva seemed to sympathize, but words are cheap and I wondered if she truly empathized with my loss. Her own maternal instincts are not much in evidence, though baby Isabella lacks nothing in the way of parental care and affection, even if the latter is mainly provided by Nathan. On this occasion though, she seems genuinely interested in probing further.

"All what? Who's to say it wouldn't work out completely differently the next time? Tom would wrap you in cotton wool. No more excursions to the barn for you..."

And that might be a pity, though it's not the main reason I'm shaking my head. "No, I'm not risking it. Never again."

"That would be a shame, because you're a natural. You and Tom would make great parents."

"Like you and Nathan, you mean?"

"Well, like Nathan. I'm still learning. But I learn fast, that's my specialty. We'll do all right. And so would you, if you take the chance."

I shake my head again. I really can't see it. Not me. Eva looks unconvinced, but she's made her point, at least for now, so she drops the matter.

I'm content to just while away the day here and nearly ignore the persistent buzzing of my phone. I'm determined not to do any work today if I can help it, and I don't immediately recognize the number calling me. I don't intend to take the call, then I relent, some instinct at work perhaps. Or maybe I feel a need to deflect Eva's attention away from my prospective motherhood, or lack of same. Whatever, I hit the green button. "Hello, Ashley McAllister…"

"Miss McAllister? It's Mr Miller. Ernest Miller, of Hampson and Miller. In Gloucester."

I think for a moment, then the penny drops. "Oh, yes, Mr Miller." It's my solicitor, the lovely old gentleman who saw me without an appointment and helped me sort out my mother's affairs. His firm now acts as my agent with the student housing folk, looking after the financial side of things and forwarding me my quarterly checks. "What can I do for you? There's nothing wrong is there?"

"Well, actually, yes. There is."

I listen quietly as he explains the reason for his call, and I have to agree. Something *has* gone very, very wrong indeed. There's been a fire, last night, at my house in Gloucester. I hear his words, try to make sense of what he's saying. Extensive damage, smoke and water, fire doors, tenants asleep inside…

"Was anyone hurt?" It's the only thing I can think of at this moment, and I desperately wrack my brains for anything else I could possibly have done to make the place safer. Did I miss something? Did I do enough?

"No, Miss McAllister. Everyone got out safely. The property's badly damaged though…"

"Safe? You say they're all safe. Are you sure?"

"Yes, I'm sure. But you'll need to talk to your insurers, and the Student Housing Team. And the fire service will want to investigate as it was a HMO..."

"A what?"

"HMO—House in Multiple Occupation. They need to check that you complied with all the fire regulations. I'm certain you did though, so nothing to worry about there. But the formalities, the process, the insurance, it's all rather complicated. Are you planning to be down here at all in the next few weeks?"

"What, yes, yes of course. I'll come. I'll be there later today. Oh, God, are you sure no one's hurt?"

"Quite sure. Today you say? I'll be here at the office all day then, let me know when you arrive."

I hang up, briefly tell Eva what's happened, and that I've got to go. To Gloucester. Now.

She agrees, but doesn't think I should be haring off alone. "What about Tom? He's out on the farm somewhere. He'll go with you. It'll be easier to sort things out if you're not on your own."

She's right, and I hit Tom's button on my speed dial. I get the unobtainable signal—he's obviously in one of the many mobile phone black spots around here, one of the perils of rural life. I leave a voicemail, and Eva promises to keep trying him as well. Thanking God or whoever else might be listening that we came over here in my car last night, I sprint for my faithful little Clio. Tom scrounged a lift from Nathan this morning so I've still got my transport. I make a brief detour to the farm to grab a bag, chuck in a few things to tide me over for a couple of days and I'm back on the road, heading for the M65.

All the way down the monotonous gray drag of the M6 and the M5, I'm turning over in my head all the things I did to try to make my house safe and fireproof. I read the regulations carefully, installed everything that was required and a lot of the additional recommendations too. I spent a bloody fortune, but it'll have been worth it if those precautions meant that my tenants survived the fire. What did Mr Miller say, they all got out safely? Did he mean no one was injured? It's at last sunk in that no one died in my house last night, but what about smoke inhalation? Horrific burns? Other terrifying images swirl around my head as all the possible disastrous consequences compete for the honor of distracting me from the road. A naturally careful driver, I give myself a talking to and get a grip. The last thing I need right now would be to find myself catapulted into the central reservation for good measure.

And accordingly, three fraught hours later, I'm pulling up outside my mother's house, my house now. Or what's left of it. I should have gone to the offices of Miller and Hampson, but my autopilot instinct brought me straight here. I need to survey the damage for myself, assure myself there isn't still some unfortunate student cowering under his bed, burnt to a crisp.

Of course the front is blackened, the door completely destroyed. There's yellow and black police crime scene tape across it, and a policeman standing solemnly beside the remains of the door. A fire service incident investigation unit van is parked in my driveway, so I assume the fire investigators are inside now. I need to talk to them, I need to know what happened. I fumble with my seat belt and manage to scramble out of the car. I walk down the path in something of a daze. My house, my beautiful house. What a mess.

"Sorry, Miss, you can't go in there." The solemn policeman places himself firmly in front of me just as I would have clambered past the police tape. I look up at him, bewildered. "But it's my house. I own it. I used to live here. I need to go in."

"Sorry, Miss, it's a crime scene. I can't let you pass."

"But..." Then it sinks in. *Crime scene.* "What crime? It was a fire. Just a fire..."

"Who did you say you are, Miss?"

"I'm Ashley, Ashley McAllister." Then, "Or Sharon Spencer. I was Sharon Spencer. My mother lived here, Susan Spencer. She died..." My voice trails off, I'm babbling. And PC Solemn is on his radio, no doubt reporting to higher authorities that a mad woman with more names than anyone should rightly lay claim to is demanding entry to his crime scene. Sure enough, he turns back to me.

"Someone will be along to talk to you soon, Miss. If you'd just like to wait here. They won't be long."

I spend the next five minutes fruitlessly quizzing PC Solemn about everything. When did it start? How did it start? How many students were inside? Where are they now? I'd have gotten more sense out of Fred and Wilma, my kittens back at Greystones. He was quite deadpan, and totally tight lipped. Always the same answer, whatever the question. "I'm sorry, Miss, I have no information I can share with you at this time."

Sure enough, reinforcements are not long in arriving. The police patrol car pulls up behind my Clio within a few minutes, and two uniformed officers swagger in my direction. I suddenly have a really bad feeling. I'm a victim, surely. My property has been attacked in some sort of as yet unspecified crime. So how come they're looking at me like something usually encountered at the bottom of a pond?

"Miss Spencer?" The first officer, a tall, stocky chap plants himself in front of me, his thumbs hooked in his ant-stab jacket and his tone definitely aggressive as he regards me down his nose.

His companion, smaller, less imposing but somewhat brighter looking if you were to ask me, is tugging his notebook out of one of his many pockets. My first reaction is just to stare at them. I know a bully when I see one. Two even. And for the life in me I can't fathom out why they're picking on me.

"Yes, I'm Sharon Spencer. Except I'm not, not any more. I'm Ashley McAllister now. I changed my name."

"Oh. And why would you want to do that then, Miss Spencer?"

"McAllister. It's Miss McAllister now." Assertive, that's what's needed, I tell myself. Polite but firm.

"I see. So, Miss Spencer, are you the owner of these premises?"

I grit my teeth, decide to let it go, for now. My instinct tells me I need to pick my battles carefully. "Yes, I told this officer"—I gesture toward my dear friend PC Solemn—"it was my mother's house, and now it's mine. She died, you see, and I inherited it. Last year."

"Yes, we've been hoping for a word with you. There are some questions we need you to answer. At the police station. Would you come with us please, Miss Spencer?"

"What, yes all right. My car's just there, in front of yours. I'll follow you."

"No, Miss Spencer, you'll come with us, in our car. Now, if you don't mind." PC Tall and Stocky is rocking on his heels, puffing out his armored chest at me, making no attempt to conceal his expression of distaste.

"What? Why?" This is all feeling horribly familiar. This is how the police spoke to me when I was arrested for lying to help Kenny. But times have changed, and I make one last attempt to get them to see reason.

"Look, I'm happy to make a statement, I want to provide any help I can. But I'll need my car later, I have to sort out insurance, see my solicitor, make arrangements for repairs..."

"There'll be no repairs for a while yet. Now, if you'd just come with us...?"

"Are you arresting me? What the hell for?"

"We were hoping it wouldn't come to that, but... Sharon Spencer, I'm arresting you on suspicion of arson..."

Chapter Five

The rest of his rights speech is lost on me as my brain turns to porridge. Arrested! I'm being bloody well arrested. For arson. These idiots think I actually set fire to my mother's house. My mother's house, for Christ's sake. My grandparents' house.

Idiots or not, I'm soon enough installed in the back of the patrol car, PC Tall and Stupid next to me while his colleague drives us to the police station. Once there, I'm taken to the custody suite, presented before the custody sergeant as an arson suspect. My panic mounting, I do at least remember enough of the drill to know I should be allowed to phone someone. At my desperate request the custody sergeant pushes the desk phone at me.

"Make it quick. We've not got all day."

Maybe I should try to get a solicitor, but the only one I know in the area is sweet old Mr Miller. This is hardly his bag. I think of Tom, because he's who I really want. I know he'll believe me, and he'll help me. But I've only got one quick phone call, and for all I know Tom's still in a mobile not-spot. I can't risk not getting through. I dial the number for Black Combe instead, and almost faint with relief when Eva answers.

"Eva, it's Ashley. Please can you get a message to Tom?"

"Ashley? Yes, of course. Where are you? Is everything all right?"

"No it's not. I've been arrested. For arson. They think I set fire to my house. With bloody students asleep inside. Christ, Eva..." My voice is cracking, she must be able to hear it. I gather my wits, I need to make sure she understands what to do. "Please could you ask Tom to arrange a solicitor for me? I have money, I can pay, but I don't know anyone. I don't know who else to call. Please, Eva..."

"Ashley, yes, it's done. Don't worry, it'll all be fine. Tom's..."

"That's enough, Miss. Time to move you along now." The custody sergeant holds out his hand for the telephone, takes it from me then hangs up. "Let's get your details and then find you a nice warm cell to wait in, shall we?"

It's not only Tom who appreciates the power of anticipation. The cell door clangs shut behind me, its note of finality echoing around me. I promised myself never again. Never, never again would I allow myself to be locked up. Yet here I am, totally innocent and even so, I spend the next hour and a half perched on the edge of a cold bench in a Spartan cell, my only other furniture a rather unsavory looking stainless steel lavatory with no seat. I make up my mind then and there I'll burst before I use that. Eventually though, the custody sergeant jangles his keys on the other side of my door and it swings open.

"Time for a little chat. Come with me please."

Numb, I get to my feet and follow him along the tiled corridor, wrinkling my nose at the putrid smell of disinfectant doing battle with vomit and pee. God, I'd just about managed to forget what these places were like. It's the smell that hits me the most, it always was. The sergeant ushers me into a small interview room where the two officers I met earlier outside my house are seated at a metal table in the middle of the room. To one side is another small table with the ubiquitous tape recorder set up on it. PC Tall and Stupid gestures for me to sit down while his colleague stands up, flicks the switch on the tape machine.

"Interview commenced at eighteen fifteen, those present PC Stuart Bragg."

Not Tall and Stupid then? I can't help thinking his official name suits him almost as well.

He turns to his colleague, still hovering beside the tape machine, who recites his name, PC George Graves. PC Bragg fixes his gaze on me. "Please state your name, for the tape."

My turn, then. "Ashley McAllister."

He glares at me, but having given my name, I remain silent. Bragg has to fill in his own gaps. "Miss McAllister, were you previously known by any other name?"

"Yes, I was. I was previously known as Sharon Spencer. But my name is now Ashley McAllister. I'd prefer it if you use my correct name please, PC Bragg. It'll be more straightforward."

He glares at me again, I'm clearly not endearing myself here. But he's got other fish to fry it seems, and decides to move on.

"Miss Spencer—McAllister, can you tell us please where you were between the hours of ten p.m. yesterday evening and four a.m. this morning?"

Well, that's simple enough. "Yes, I had dinner with friends."

"Friends? Do these 'friends' have names, Miss McAllister?"

"They do." I rattle off Tom, Nathan and Eva's names, and provide their contact details too. Upstanding citizens all, company directors and a doctor of something or other. Eva's a doctor of several something or others in fact. At least my alibi should stand up to scrutiny.

Undaunted, PC Tall and Stupid, sorry, Bragg, presses on with his line of inquiry. Line of total and crass idiocy if you ask me, but still, if there were prizes to be had for effort and determination, he'd be in the center of the podium. "Earlier, when you were arrested, you mentioned needing to contact your insurers. Do you remember that, Miss McAllister?"

"Of course."

"Could you tell us the details of your insurance, Miss McAllister? How much do you stand to gain as a result of this fire?"

Ah, so that's it. The penny drops. They think this is some sort of insurance scam. I could almost laugh out loud it's so totally ridiculous. "No, I don't know the insurance details. I need to dig out my policy, talk to the insurance company. I expect the repairs should be covered though."

"Unless the fire was started deliberately, Miss McAllister. That would make your insurance void, would it not?"

So this is what they meant by a crime scene. "Was it started deliberately? If so, how?"

"You tell us, Miss McAllister."

"I know nothing about how the fire started. The first I knew of it was when my solicitor phoned me this morning. That's Mr Miller at Miller and Hampson. They handle things for me, collect the rent and so on. I don't live in this area anymore."

He makes a point of studying the papers in front of him, including the personal details taken down by the custody sergeant. "And where is it you live now? Greystones, West Yorkshire. You're a long way from home."

"Yes. Because my solicitor phoned me to tell me that my house, the house I grew up in, the house that belonged to my mother, and to my grandparents before her, had been on fire. I was worried. I wanted to see the damage for myself. I wanted to start putting it right. And I was concerned about my tenants, the students. Someone could have been killed. Or seriously hurt. So yes, I *am* a long way from home." I speak with deliberate care. He really is incredibly dim, and from me that's saying something.

We glare at each other across the battered metal table, antagonism bristling between us. I know I should be more…servile…but these days I reserve that for Tom. It's more rewarding. Long, hostile moments pass as we stare each other down, then the tension is broken by a tap at the door. PC Graves steps outside for a moment then comes back to whisper in Tall and Stupid's ear. He listens, flicks his eyes up at me then gets to his feet.

"It seems your solicitor's here. We'll leave you alone for a few minutes." He heads for the door, but has to step back sharply to avoid being barreled aside by the most imperious woman I think I've ever seen. She is one seriously scary lady, very tall, slim and austerely dressed in a dark gray closely fitted suit, a white blouse and four-inch black patent leather heels. Her fingernails are painted a brilliant red to match her lips.

Her hair is pale blonde, pulled back into a severe chignon. She turns her head slightly to view the retreating police officers with thinly disguised contempt.

"I'll summon you when my briefing with my client is complete. Thank you." And so they are dismissed, and she turns her attention to me. Coming forward she places her elegant burgundy leather briefcase on the table before offering me one perfectly manicured hand. "You'll be Ashley McAllister. I'm Julia Montgomery, from Jones Montgomery Sheldon. I'm representing you today."

Well, she certainly looks the part. And I'm incredibly pleased to see her. "I, er, thank you. Did Tom send you?"

She fixes me with a formidable stare, assessing me. I shift uncomfortably, but she relents and explains her presence here. "I believe Mr Shore is on his way to Gloucester, as is Mr Darke. However, my services *were* retained by Darke Associates, though it was Miss Byrne who instructed me in this matter. My firm handles most of their legal work, although predominantly in matters of property and civil law. However, the occasional foray into criminal proceedings does help to keep the account interesting. Now, shall we press on, Miss McAllister?"

Interesting? Well that's me all right. I settle back, ready to do whatever's needed to get me out of here. Darke Associates? Nathan's corporate legal team? They should be up to the job. And it seems I have Eva—Miss Byrne—to thank for sending me Ms Montgomery. I turn my attention to the efficient solicitor who is deftly unscrewing the top of her elegant fountain pen, poised to take notes.

"So, tell me about the premises where this incident took place. The house was formerly your mother's home, I understand, which you inherited a year ago. Is that correct?"

"Yes, that's right." I go on to explain to her about not wanting to sell the house, for sentimental reasons as much as anything, but also because I saw a real chance to get a decent commercial return out if it.

"So, you own the freehold. Was there any outstanding borrowing against it when it came into your possession?"

"No, my grandparents bought it originally, back in the mid-sixties I think, when they got married. The mortgage was paid off years ago."

"I see. And what about you? How did you finance the renovation and conversion works? Did you borrow against the value of the premises?"

"No. I could have I suppose, but I paid for the work out of the rest of my inheritance. As well as the house I got around fifty thousand in cash. So that's what I used."

"You spent fifty thousand pounds on the refurbishment costs? That sounds like a lot." Her glance up from her notes is sharp, her tone clipped. I get the impression these details are extremely important so I think carefully about the work I did on the house, try to explain my reasons for spending so much. "I saw it as an investment. I had to put in bathrooms, extra kitchen facilities. And fire escapes. Christ, I'm glad of those now. And fire resistant doors, a wired in alarm system. The council building control inspector made me move the downstairs sensor three times before he was happy. And you're right, it did cost a lot. But I reckon I'll get my money back within about another four years. Could even do it in three."

"I see. Can you explain to me your financial forecasting then, an outline of your business model?"

"My what? What do you mean?"

She smiles at me, just a little less frostily. "Your sums, Miss McAllister. How do you calculate you'll have your money back within four years?"

"Oh, right. I see. Well, the rent from student lets will be at least sixteen thousand a year, after agents' fees and other expenses. Could be as much as twenty if the place is let out over the summer as well—conferences, summer schools, that sort of thing. But assuming not, just sixteen. I've had just over eight thousand so far this year so that's on target. If the lettings continue at that level I'll be in profit in three years, but I'm being cautious. I think four's a safe estimate. Especially now, as the house won't be fit to let again for at least a few weeks so I'll lose money until it's fixed."

She's nodding, rapidly scribbling notes on a yellow solicitor's notepad.

"I'm assuming you can account for your whereabouts last night?"

"Yes, I can." I explain that I was with Tom, and we stayed overnight at Nathan Darke's home.

She seems satisfied with that. "Right. The preliminary reports from the fire investigation department suggest that an accelerant was used." She explains further at my puzzled expression, "Petrol. Poured through the letterbox in all probability. That's why most of the damage is in the hallway and the front door. The internal fire doors protected the rest of the house, pretty much, until the fire service arrived and put it out."

Even though I knew it had to be something like this I'm still shocked. "Petrol. Someone poured petrol through the letterbox and set it alight. Knowing there were people asleep inside. Oh, God…" I drop my face into my hands, feeling sick suddenly. It could so easily have been an absolute tragedy.

Ms Montgomery waits for a few moments, apparently considering, then leans over the table, takes my hands in both of hers, squeezes and tugs until I look up at her. She holds my gaze, the glint of steel shimmering in her dark gray eyes. "You did a good job, Miss McAllister. Ashley. Your high quality refurbishment, in particular your fire safety works, probably saved your property. And may well have saved lives too. Now, though, I need you to think. We know you didn't pour petrol through that letterbox, but someone did. Have you any idea who might have done it? Have you any enemies? Anyone with a grudge?"

The obvious candidate is Kenny, so I briefly explain my previous association with him. But for all I know he's still in jail. And anyway, this just isn't his sort of thing. He's a thug, handy with his fists, but to plan an arson attack? And manage to carry it out? He'd be more likely to set himself on fire. I can't really see it and I tell her so. She nods, but even so uses her iPad to email her clerk with instructions to ascertain whether Kenny is on the loose again.

It seems to me there's another, more obvious, explanation. "Ms Montgomery, surely, it's more likely the target would be one of the students, not me. Have the police looked into that, checked out their backgrounds?"

"We'll definitely put that to them. It they haven't properly eliminated other reasonable possibilities that would weaken their case considerably if this does end up in court."

My heart lurches, the reality of my predicament suddenly in sharp focus, all the hellish implications of the situation becoming clear. I gaze at her, wide-eyed.

"Oh, God, do you think it'll come to that?" Given my record, my suspended sentence and the terms of my parole I have visions of being remanded in custody, I could be back in my old cell at HMP Eastwood Park before the day's out. It was bearable before, but it wouldn't be this time. This time I'm innocent, and I've got a life. A brilliant new life that I'm fast realizing could easily come crashing down around me unless the indomitable Ms Montgomery can make PC Tall and Stupid see sense. I desperately wish Tom was here, he'd know what to do, what to say, but I gather he's on his way. Nathan too. And meanwhile they've sent Ms Montgomery to get between me and disaster. She seems to know her stuff, she's calm, confident, and I can't help thinking that if I'd had her on my side a year ago I'd never have become so intimately acquainted with the interior decoration at Eastwood Park.

She looks at me, controlled, poised, properly briefed and ready to take on PC Bragg. She smiles at me, nods briskly as she assembles her papers into a neat pile in front of her. "Now," she announces, business-like, crisp, "now, we make this go away."

Brisk and ready for the coming fight, she stands, goes to the door and knocks smartly on it. "We're ready."

Chapter Six

"PC Bragg, my client had neither motive nor opportunity to commit this offense. I insist that you release her immediately."

PC Bragg's response is to lean casually back in his chair, surveying the pair of us with a blend of arrogance and contempt. "Motive? Your client's motive was greed. Money, pure and simple. She made sure she had the property insured then she set it alight to make a claim. She showed total disregard for her tenants sleeping inside. We're heading for an attempted murder charge here, Mrs Montgomery. Your client's going to be with us for a long time yet and she'd better get used to that fact and start telling me the truth."

"PC Bragg, what do you know of cash flow forecasting, profit margins, commercial rate of return? And specifically, given the performance to date of Miss McAllister's investment, how do you arrive at the conclusion that she would gain financially from such an act? On the contrary, would it not have constituted financial suicide?"

"Eh?"

She gives him no opportunity to regroup. "I thought you probably hadn't considered the fiscal implications, or you wouldn't be pursuing this ridiculous line of inquiry. Let me explain. Miss McAllister invested the sum of fifty thousand pounds one year ago to convert the property for student accommodation. She was particularly diligent with regard to fire safety, and that diligence has without doubt saved her tenants from serious injury or even death. She is an exemplary landlord and an astute business woman."

Me? Does she mean me?

Not to be so easily thrown off the scent, PC Bragg indicates his interest in knowing where I acquired fifty grand from, just to be airily dismissed by Ms Montgomery, clearly not about to waste overmuch time on his fantasy world. "Miss McAllister inherited that sum, which is a matter of public record easily verified by reference to the Court of Probate. I'm sure you are perfectly familiar with the law in this regard, constable."

The constable's eyes narrow angrily as he bristles at the slur, but he can't quite find a way to retaliate effectively. In any case, Julia Montgomery ignores him, pressing on with her annihilation of his so-called case.

"Miss McAllister calculated her rate of return based upon around sixty percent occupancy which will see her initial investment returned to her within four years. A more normal, and perfectly acceptable term would be ten years, so Miss McAllister's investment was a particularly prudent one."

Me? Prudent? I'm liking the sound of this.

"In fact, the performance of her investment has been well in excess of Miss McAllister's initial business model. Her property has achieved occupancy rates of nearer to eighty percent, which would see her in profit within three years. Far from having a financial incentive to see the property go up in flames, she stands to lose money as a result of this unfortunate incident. Put those commercial realities alongside the fact that this house holds considerable sentimental value to my client. The house has been in her family for three generations. It was her grandparents' home. Her mother grew up there, as did Miss McAllister herself. If she wanted to raise cash, she could have sold the property when it came into her possession a year ago, but she chose not to because she wanted to keep it. Instead, she invested her own funds in improving and converting her old home, turned it into a lucrative business venture. No, constable, you will have to look elsewhere for a motive."

"She had plenty of opportunity..."

"No, she did not. Miss McAllister has accounted for her movements. No doubt you will have taken steps to verify her alibi for last night?"

Looking somewhat deflated now, PC Bragg's surly expression suggests that he has indeed received word from the West Yorkshire police that my alibi is solid. Once more, I suspect I have Eva to thank, her impeccable credentials as a respected academic and doctor of just about everything no doubt doing no harm at all to my case. What it is to have powerful friends. Friends who'll send you hot shot lawyers and speak up for you when it matters.

We're on the downhill slope now—PC Bragg's idiotic assertions crumbling before our eyes. Ms

Montgomery again insists that I be released, and this time he offers no objections.

On reflection it was not a fair fight. Not even close. Julia Montgomery wiped the floor with PC Tall and Stupid. I doubt he even knew what hit him. Every one of his inane suggestions had been obliterated by her cool, incisive arguments, her clipped tones making a mockery of his bullying swagger and half-baked innuendo. His face was a particular joy to watch as he tried to make sense of this force of nature now confronting him, challenging all his preconceived certainties and leaving him looking more than faintly ridiculous. I'd have laughed out loud if the whole matter was not so very serious for me. Still, I can appreciate a bit of sport as much as the next person, and Ms Montgomery certainly seemed to enjoy herself as she took his flimsy case apart.

His original assessment of me was that I'm some cheap little ex-con who must have done this because, as far as he could work out, nothing else made sense? So he never considered any other possibility. As Julia Montgomery made absolutely clear to him, that was a big mistake.

* * * *

Ten minutes later I'm walking down the front steps of the police station, the wonderful Ms Montgomery marching smugly beside me. I get the impression she's thoroughly enjoyed herself, slumming in Gloucester. At the bottom of the steps I turn to shake her hand once more, to thank her.

"My pleasure, Miss McAllister. Can I drop you anywhere?"

I'm about to thank her, a lift back to my old house to pick up my car would be very helpful, when a voice behind me has me whirling.

"No need for that. Ashley has transport."

I turn, and with a screech of welcome launch myself into Tom's arms. He catches me, swings me around as I grab his wonderful, handsome, laughing face between my hands and kiss his lips. I was pleased to see Julia Montgomery, but I'm absolutely delighted to see Tom. I hug him, my arms around his neck as he turns to acknowledge my savior, still poised elegantly at the foot of the police station steps.

"Julia, how lovely to see you. And looking formidable as ever. Thanks for your help today. I owe you."

"You're welcome. It's just fortunate I was down here today visiting my old school in Cheltenham when I received Miss Byrne's call. And what you owe me is my fee, which will, of course, not be inconsiderable. I'll send you an invoice." She smiles at him, and I catch a glimmer of something intimate flash between them. These two obviously know each other.

"Of course, and worth every penny." He leans forward, kisses her lightly on the cheek. "It's good to know you're not losing your touch."

She smiles, her face now genuinely warm with real friendship. "I rather enjoyed myself, although I think the police case would have collapsed soon enough. The CPS would have thrown it out. I just speeded things up, and it was much more exciting than the usual stuff you two wheel me out for. Which reminds me, where is the delectable Nathan? Eva told me he was with you."

"Parking the car. He'll be along in a moment."

"I see. Well, I really do need to get off, so just tell him I asked after him will you? Maybe I'll run into him at the club. You too. Bye for now, and it was nice to meet you properly, Miss McAllister." She bustles away, slipping confidently into a smart BMW parked in a reserved space. With a polite wave, she cruises past us and out into the stream of traffic.

"What did she mean, properly? I've never met her before. I'd have definitely remembered."

"I expect it's just that she looks different with her clothes on. Same as you do, my darling." He laughs softly at my incredulous expression, swings an arm across my shoulders as he starts to lead me away across the police station forecourt. "Jules was at The Hermitage that first night we went there. She found your, er—your performance in the dungeon particularly inspiring. I gather her sub got quite a working over after that…"

I stop, stare at him, astonished. No. Surely not! My mouth is hanging open, and Tom casually hooks his finger under my chin to close it.

"Small world, love. Jules is a Domme. A Mistress, if you like. And she's a powerful one, very stern. Scary woman. Bloody good lawyer though."

"Shit. No wonder she kicked that stupid policeman in the balls then, figuratively speaking, of course. Christ, she made mincemeat out of him."

"Good. That's what we wanted. Now, where's Nathan?"

Right on cue the sleek black Porsche slides around the corner and pulls up on yellow lines outside the police station. Tom opens the door and ushers me into the back seat, sliding in alongside me. Nathan pulls away. "So, how's our little jailbird then? I'm guessing the lovely Jules did her stuff and sprung you?"

Nathan tosses the cheery greeting over his shoulder at me.

"Yes. She was wonderful. She sends her regards, by the way."

He just nods, his attention back on the traffic. "So, where to?"

I think for a moment, then, "Could we go to my mother's house? My car's there. And then I need to see Mr Miller. He's my solicitor who handles my financial affairs here. But he'll have gone home by now. I suppose I'll need to find a hotel and go to his office tomorrow."

Tom takes my hand, squeezes it. "Hotel's sorted, love. We've got rooms booked at the Gloucester Marriott. For tonight at least. Tomorrow we'll decide if we're staying on or what. After we've spoken to your Mr Miller."

I turn to him, my gratitude etched across my face. "You're staying? With me?"

"Too right we're staying." This from Nathan, "You need some moral support."

"And a decent fuck, but that's my department."

Tom's whisper in my ear sends a wicked shiver down my spine, and I have to concentrate hard on giving Nathan directions back to my mother's house.

My Clio's still outside where I left it, but my heart sinks when I spot the broken driver's window as we draw up in front of it.

"Shit. That's all I need. Someone's broken into my car."

Tom's equally disgusted, though for different reasons. "And in full view of half the bloody Gloucester constabulary too. What sort of a place is this?"

I'm close to tears as I stand helplessly on the pavement, viewing the pile of shattered glass on the driver's seat, and the contents of my glove box scattered all over the passenger side. It's a mess, and I'm going to need to get it fixed before I can go anywhere. But at least my car's still here. They could have stolen it. In fact, I'm a bit puzzled about why they didn't. Why bother going to the trouble of breaking in just to rummage through my glove box? They didn't even nick my CDs — obviously not devotees of Coldplay and Amy Winehouse. But still, it seems odd.

Efficient as ever, Nathan's on the phone sorting out a mobile windscreen repair firm offering a twenty-four hour service. It seems I'll be good as new again within an hour or so. And Tom's marching up the path to my wrecked front door, the twisted, scorched uPVC now just a melted tangle. PC Solemn is gone, but the police tape is still in place. They've also arranged a boarding up firm to secure a couple of stout wooden planks across the doorway, to keep out prying eyes and no doubt to preserve evidence for the investigators. None of whom are in evidence now. The place is deserted, lonely and abandoned. And that does it for me. I follow Tom to the door, powerfully reminded of another time I walked up this path, alone on that occasion. It was the day I was released from prison, and I came home looking for my mother even though I knew she wasn't here anymore. I found Sadie then, and now she's gone too, and someone even tried to destroy my house. On that thought I turn, sit on the step, put my head in my hands and weep.

And suddenly, Tom's arms are around me. He's sitting beside me, holding me. He doesn't say anything, no useless soothing words, no attempt to stop my tears as the dam bursts and the grief and tension of this awful day flow from me. The shock and terror of this morning when I heard what had happened, and feared that people might have died because of me. Then the desperate rush to drive down here, the shock of actually seeing the damage to my lovely house then the sickening realization that some evil git did this on purpose, someone deliberately tried to burn my house to the ground. Then the horror of realizing the police believed that evil person was me, that I could do such a terrible thing. But then came Julia, sent by Eva. And Tom and Nathan actually followed me, came here to help me, because they knew I needed them. Like some sort of desperate limpet, I cling to Tom, his hands tracing circling caresses on my back as my sobs eventually subside. I sniff into his neck, trying not to leave nasty marks on his clean sports shirt.

"Here. Use this."

I turn, to see Nathan crouching in front of us, a clean hanky in his hand. It's one of those nice, fancy ones. Real fabric. Seems a pity to wipe my nose on it, but that doesn't stop me. I dab at my eyes, blow my nose noisily. I consider offering him the handkerchief back but think better of it and shove it into my pocket to wash later. I look from one to the other, my gaze still watery. I'm fragile, but ready to start picking myself up. And I know that this time, it'll be so much easier with people around to help me. This time, it's not just me against the world. I start to smile, wobbly, but near enough.

The smile dies at the sound of a voice, a sneering, coarse, cruel voice, a voice I'd hoped never to hear again.

"Well, isn't this nice. Who're your ponsy friends then, Shaz?"

Chapter Seven

Kenny's leaning on my gatepost, his hands in his pockets. Or should I say, Tom's pockets. He's wearing Tom's leather jacket, the one he stole on the river bank in Bristol, although to be fair it looks faintly ridiculous on him, at least three sizes too big. And he's smiling, an unpleasant smirk signaling distinctly malicious intent. And he's not alone. There's a white Transit van parked on the other side of the street, and I count five other thugs pouring out of the open rear doors, coming across to arrange themselves around Kenny. One of them is even trying the doors of Nathan's Porsche, the others just lounging arrogantly against our cars. A man I recognize as one of Kenny's vicious mates from way back in Bristol—his broken nose and tattooed face particularly memorable—saunters up behind Kenny, swinging a bicycle chain, his intent obvious. He grins at us, clearly enjoying his day out in Gloucester and convinced it's about to get a whole lot better.

I'm starting to get up, ready to try to reason with him even though I know it's useless. Old habits do die hard, it seems.

"Kenny isn't it? How nice. I'd been hoping to run into you again." Tom has taken over, before I can say anything to Kenny. His voice is mocking, confident. This is my Dom, but more so. This is Tom looking for trouble, real trouble. And no doubt about to find it. Can't he count? Six, for Christ sake!

"You have something of mine." Tom makes no effort to stand up, and his arms around me hold me firmly in place. He fixes Kenny with a warning look, a look I know well but which seems to be lost on my ex-boyfriend. "I'd like my jacket back please."

"Who the fuck are you?" Kenny takes a menacing step forward, his loyal troops coming to attention behind him, ready now to have their fun beating up two unarmed men and a weeping girl.

"We'll sort this. Stay here," Tom murmurs his instructions into my ear as he lazily comes to his feet. Nathan too, and they stroll casually down the path to meet Kenny head on.

"We met a couple of years ago. In Bristol as I recall. You — borrowed — my jacket, and I see you still have it. It definitely looks better on me — you don't really fill it out. Prison food not especially good for the physique, I expect. And now I want it back." Tom's tone is low, hard, chilling. He's angry, white-hot angry. I've heard that tone only once before, that first day in Smithy's Forge. He means business. But he and Nathan are hopelessly outnumbered. Ever the optimist, I expect they'll land a few decent punches before it's all done with. I can't see them winning this one though, then my immediate future looks distinctly grim. After all, it's not Tom and Nathan that Kenny's come here looking for—it's me.

Kenny's lips curls into a sneer. "Looks like you borrowed my shagbag." He casts a contemptuous nod in my direction, turns back to Tom. "I reckon I got the best of the bargain, but now I'll be needing the little slag back."

He turns his attention to me, his eyes glinting with a mixture of cruelty and something akin to lust, but tinged with violence, greedy and assessing.

I don't recall sensing such an aura of menace from him at any time in our previous relationship, but something fundamental has shifted and it's unmistakable now. Scared, really scared, I shrink backwards. He obviously notices my reaction, and his sneer widens, becomes yet more malevolent as he senses my fear, feeds on it, enjoys it.

He turns his arrogant attention back to Nathan and Tom, dismissive as he warns them off. "You two can fuck off. Last chance. It's her we want." Then, his attention is back to me, "Yeah, you. You treacherous little bitch. You couldn't keep your fucking mouth shut could you? You grassed us up, I got three fucking years because of you, so you fucking know what's coming to you…"

He starts to laugh, turning to his crew to share the joke. He very nearly makes it before Tom's fist connects with his jaw, sending him spinning backwards into the loving arms of his friend with the bike chain. Then all hell breaks loose. Kenny's not frankly much use for anything anymore. One decent punch and he's floored. That leaves just five.

Just?

The others are made of sterner stuff, but it soon becomes obvious they've miscalculated. Nathan moves like lightning, high kicks and punishing jabs flying everywhere. *Nathan the Ninja, wow!* And Tom's something of a bruiser too, fast and lethal and not above fighting a bit dirty when he gets the chance. A fierce kick in Kenny's ribs as he's lying on the pavement is obviously intended to settle old scores, and I can't say I blame him.

A couple of minutes, no more than that, and there are three more would-be heroes rolling in the muck alongside the noble Kenny, and the other two are backing away, obviously no longer so keen on the day's entertainment. He of the bicycle chain is among the fallen, and Nathan uncoils the chain from around his pudgy, tattooed hand, clearly intending to make sure he doesn't get to wrap it around anyone else's head any time soon.

Tom, meanwhile, is intent on hauling Kenny into a sitting position and he deftly pulls his arms through the sleeves of the jacket. It's seen a lot of wear, in fact it's distinctly tatty now and I have no doubt that Tom won't be wearing it again. It's a point of principle though, and the jacket, newly restored to its rightful owner is soon stowed in the boot of the Porsche along with the bike chain.

"Right, you lot can fuck off and take that pile of shite with you." Nodding casually in the direction of Kenny and the other three fallen heroes, Nathan's tone is as hard and implacable as Tom's, and I begin to appreciate how formidable he must be when in Dom mode. I bet Eva loves it. These guys though, are just plain cowards, bullies with the tables turned, and they can't get away from us fast enough. Not especially gently they drag their fallen comrades to their feet and the whole pack of them shuffle off back across the street to bundle their semi-conscious colleagues back into their van and clamber in behind them.

The least battered limps around to the front and hauls himself into the driver's seat, offering a two finger salute in passing to Mrs Whatsername, my mother's old next door neighbor. She's ventured as far as her front door to watch the goings on and from the expression of utter disgust on her face is no doubt silently noting that Norman's mother would never have caused such a commotion in the street. I can't help thinking she'd have been better employed calling the police rather than watching from her doorstep, but I suppose it was all over so quickly it hardly seems worth it now. By way of peace-making, as we all watch the van lurching down the road, Tom offers her a cheery "Good evening" before she nips back inside a bit sharpish and slams the door on us all.

As Kenny and co. disappear around the corner, my instinct is to make a run for it, to get away. I can't believe we're still alive, let alone all of us standing around as if nothing much has happened.

"You could have been killed. Both of you…" I'm staring from one to the other as they casually check over Nathan's Porsche for any mucky finger marks in the gleaming black paintwork. "Christ, there were six of them…"

"Mmm, decent odds this time. I'm glad I had him to back me up, especially as my ribs are still a bit delicate." Tom smiles at Nathan. "Thanks, mate, I owe you one."

"You're welcome. Any time." Nathan crouches to check his tires.

"Six, for God's sake. Can't either of you count?"

"Yes, six. Same as the number of dans on his black belt. The Karate Kid here." Again he nods in Nathan's direction, who seems quite oblivious to my concerns as he now checks his lights. "Mind, I always knew he'd come in useful in a scrap. I'd have been a lot more nervous on my own. Like before, in Bristol."

Karate? Black belt? Bloody hell. Kenny's little band of numpties wouldn't have known what hit them. Nathan scattered them like skittles. And even though, in fairness, Nathan did do most of the work, Tom was pretty lethal himself. For old times' sake I don't doubt. As my heart rate at last settles down into a more sedate canter I notice that his knuckles are scratched — no doubt Kenny's chin is in worse shape though. He smiles, rubs his sore knuckles ruefully as he sees where my gaze has landed.

"It was worth it. Been wanting to do that for two years. Life's good sometimes, don't you think?"

I can't help but smile back. "Yes, sometimes, and now at least you've got your jacket back."

He pulls me into his arms, drops a quick kiss on my mouth. "This was not about a jacket, sweetheart. This was more about me fucking hating that little shit. For what he did to you."

No one except my mother has ever defended me before, and I find I rather like it. I have a champion, two champions even. But now it's over, thank God, and we need to get out of here. I tug at Tom's sleeve, desperate to get him back in the Porsche. "Come on, we need to get moving. They might be back. They'll probably bring even more next time."

Tom's not for running away, and apparently sees no need for undue haste. "They won't be back. Do you suppose they're going to tell the rest of their old cellmates that they got beaten up by two 'ponsy' blokes? All six of them? Nah, they're done. And hey, like you say, I got my jacket back. I call that a result."

"Yeah, and I got a bike chain. I'm sure I can think of a good use for that..."

Nathan looks thoughtful, and I wonder what Eva's reaction to his new toy might be. He'll have to get it cleaned up a bit first.

Then, all business as usual, Nathan's strolling round to lean casually on the bonnet of his Porsche. "So, where were we? Right, Autoglass should be here soon. We'll just wait until they show up, and as soon as your car's fixed we'll go to the Marriott and get cleaned up. Maybe grab something to eat. How's that sound?"

It still sounds to me as though we're pushing our luck hanging around here, but Tom seems as unruffled as Nathan, so we stay.

Tom loops an arm across my shoulders, squeezes lightly. "Hey, come on. They've gone, they won't be back. You're safe enough now."

I realize I'm shivering, the shock of the encounter just now starting to get to me.

Tom continues, "Well it's pretty clear now who broke into your car I'd say. And maybe the fire too... Seems too much of a coincidence for him to just turn up here, don't you think? He's quite a long way from his old stomping ground surely..."

"I didn't even know he was out." My voice is quiet, barely more than a whisper. I'd been dreading ever meeting up with Kenny again, and the fact that he's come all the way here, to Gloucester, means he's definitely been looking for me. Gone to all the trouble of tracking me down. And to bring so many mates, all of them apparently intent on finding me. I feel my heart lurch as the implications sink in. Oh God, suppose he knows? Suppose he's figured it out... His words are still ringing around my head. 'Grass' 'What's coming to you'.

Oh, yes, he definitely knows.

"You okay, love?" There's concern in Tom's voice as he tips my chin up with his fingers to study my face. "You're pale. And you're shaking. Come and sit down."

I'm quickly installed in the passenger seat of the Porsche, a bottle of chilled water in my hand, whilst Tom and Nathan continue to confer on the pavement. They're both looking puzzled, and I can't say I blame them. None of this makes much sense. Not to them anyway.

Soon enough the Autoglass repair van pulls up behind us and the cheery mechanic in lurid green overalls hops out to inspect the damage. "Soon have you on your way, sir," he promises Tom, who doesn't bother to disillusion him regarding the Clio's ownership.

And sure enough, within another half an hour the glass is replaced and he's punching my insurance details into his tablet computer, the deal done. I'm still more than a bit frayed around the edges so Tom takes my keys and drives my car, and I hunch myself up in the passenger seat, willing him not to ask me any questions. Mercifully he doesn't, and twenty more minutes sees the three of us checking into the Marriott.

Tom and I head off into our room, after arranging to meet Nathan in the restaurant downstairs in a couple of hours. I'm hoping the decent fuck Tom promised me might be on the near horizon—I really need something a bit special right now to distract me from the thoughts and bone-deep fears whirling around inside my skull. First though, I need to rinse away the grimy feeling left on my clothes and body from my visit to the police station and close encounter with my previous nemesis. I head for the shower while Tom kicks off his shoes and flings himself onto the bed to wait.

Not a man known for his patience, at least in matters relating to the physical, it's not long before I hear the swish of the shower curtain behind me, and Tom joins me in the warm spray. His hands are gentle, efficient, as he shampoos and conditions my hair, raking his fingers through its length to ease out the day's tangles before rinsing it thoroughly. Next, he deftly peels the wrapper off a tiny bar of hotel soap and washes my back, my still slightly tender bottom, my legs. Then he reaches around me to smooth the lather into my breasts and belly. He pays particularly keen attention to the professionally waxed smooth skin at the apex of my thighs. I sigh and lean back as he slips his fingers expertly between the soft, slick inner lips to circle the entrance to my pussy. His touch feels good, at first relaxing me rather than arousing, the intent to calm and reassure as much as to incite my response. Still, inevitably, my pleasure mounts, slowly, surely. I sigh, then gasp. I give a soft moan as he slides first one then two fingers inside me, the heel of his hand carefully angled to rub my clit. Soft at first, he increases the pressure as my moans become hectic little pants, as I tighten my grip on his forearms. My body stiffens, readying itself for the delicious release I know is close. Suddenly, it's there and I'm spinning, my body convulsing around the gentle, probing fingers, my muscles melting. I gasp his name, would crumble but for his arms holding me now, and he murmurs in my ear, his words to do with love, and being there, and holding me safe.

When I'm still and calm again, my legs at last capable of supporting my weight, Tom kisses my neck before stepping out of the shower and reaching for one of the large hotel towels piled in a pristine white fluffy bale on the bathroom floor. I watch him, somewhat surprised and mildly disappointed not to have found myself up against the tiled wall, his cock deep inside me. He fastens the towel around his hips, knotting it loosely before picking up another and holding it wide open for me to step into. I do so, still not certain where this new format is taking us as he wraps me carefully, tucking the ends in tight, all neat and decent and prim.

"You didn't— I mean, don't you want to…"

"I promised you a decent fuck, and you'll get it. In time. Be patient. I always deliver, you know that, Ashley. First though, we talk." And with that he grabs another, smaller towel to twist around my hair, turban-style. Mostly—and most especially when we're naked—he's my big, tough, hard Dom, demanding and stern, with the power to hurt and delight me in equal measure. And occasionally, just occasionally, he reminds me of my mother.

Chapter Eight

A few moments later we're sitting on the end of the big double bed in our hotel room, Tom behind me as he pulls me onto his lap and works his fingers again through my hair, squeezing the wet into the towel before grabbing a wide-toothed comb to gently ease out the tangles. I admire his reflection, our reflection, in the mirror over the dressing table directly ahead. He's intent on his task, and I take the opportunity to study him, his blond hair still wet and messy from being roughly toweled, his damp torso deliciously sculpted, hard and firm, glistening from the shower, his muscles clearly defined as he reaches around me to pull the damp hair back from my forehead. My Dom, gloriously beautiful in a way that I'm convinced very few men can ever achieve, rough and raw and cruelly efficient when he uses pain to focus my attention, yet achingly tender when he chooses to be. Like now.

He glances up, catches my gaze in the mirror, holds it. I am struck by the physical contrast between us — his blond good looks, his hard, chiseled body, vivid green eyes. I particularly love Tom's healthy tan, gained from an outdoor existence rather than more sedentary sun worshiping, darker on his hands and arms, his legs and feet much paler, covered invariably by jeans and boots. And me, dark eyes, olive complexion, the same skin tone everywhere as I hate uncovering outdoors, my build fragile in comparison to Tom, but I like to think wiry and resilient for all that, my hair so dark as to be almost black. Tom smiles at me, winks and returns to his task as I continue to observe his actions reflected in the mirror.

"You know that I love you, don't you, Ashley?"

What? My eyes snap back up, and he's watching me, his expression soft but an unmistakable glint of determination shimmering in those emerald eyes. I stare back at him, amazed. He's never said that to me before. He's texted it, shown me it in many, many ways. But never actually come right out and said it.

"Don't you?" The question again, requiring a response.

"I—yes, I know that. But you never say it."

"Not in those exact words maybe. But I do say it. I say it when I touch you, kiss you, when I wake up next to you. You knew." His tone is quiet, soft, but certain. And he's right. I did know. I nod, and he smiles at my reflection.

"And you trust me, yes?"

"Yes." *Definitely. Emphatically.* Again I nod.

"Then tell me what's behind all this." He's stopped combing my hair, and he's just maintaining eye contact with me in the mirror, quietly waiting.

I drop my eyes first, but he's having none of that. He slips his fingers under my chin to lift my face up, his words in my ear insist I look at him.

"Tell me. Tell me why Kenny's so determined to come after you. What's between you and him still?"

"Nothing. Nothing, I swear!" My heated, panicked denial just draws a wry smile from him.

"No, love, I don't mean that. You're all mine now. I know that. But there's something, something from before, something that means he's not letting go. He torched your house, and for all he knew you might have been inside it. Or maybe he thought your mother was— Does he know she died? He broke into your car. *Your* car. He came all the way to Gloucester looking for you, knew just where to find you. He talked about you getting what was coming to you. He brought a vanload of mates. If you'd been alone today at the house when he turned up with his gang of thugs—you'd have been in the back of that van, love. That was an attempted abduction, you know it, I know it, Nathan too. And Christ knows what would have happened to you, it doesn't bear thinking about. So, why? What's it all about?"

He's on it. Spot on. I grasp around for some straw or other, anything to throw him off the scent. "Maybe, maybe he just…wants me back…"

Tom shrugs, the slight shake of his head dispelling any optimism I might have had that he'd be satisfied with my explanation. "Well that might account for it if he was a just shade brighter. And if he hadn't brought a small army with him. But we both know he lacks any finer feelings, never appreciated you when he had you. If he just wanted someone to fuck he'd have moved on, found someone else by now. Probably has, in fact. So no, I'm not buying that. There's more. I want to know what that 'more' is. And I want to know now."

His voice has hardened, his words still quiet, no hint of anger, but determination is there. That solid core of steely resolve honed to perfection by years as a

Dominant. And recognizing that, I can't quite control that trace of self-destructive devilment that drives me to bait him.

"Or what? You'll spank me?"

"What a lovely idea. Would that help?" His polite response belies the underlying threat.

"It usually gets my attention, helps me to focus…"

"Worth considering then, as Plan B. We'll come back to that. But first, I'm just asking. Asking you because I love you and I want you to trust me, to let me help you. Tell me about Kenny, tell me why he's still coming after you. Why would he have tried to abduct you today?" That tone, low, no hint of anger, but resolved, implacable. He's not giving up, never giving up. He knows I'm lying, evading.

"Ashley, tell me now. All of it. Now." His hands are in my hair, holding my head up, forcing me to meet his gaze in the mirror, steady, solid, both terrifying and at the same time reassuring, a bizarre contradiction of tenderness and force, turbulence and safe harbor. Irresistible.

I breathe deeply, close my eyes, and he shakes me, the movement tiny but sharp, insisting. I open my eyes, come back to him and obey his command.

"David. It was David."

He relaxes his grip on me, nuzzles my ear, kisses me. If he's surprised at my answer he doesn't show it. And he instantly knows what I'm talking about. "David, your baby. Yes. Go on…"

So I do go on, "When David died, I blamed myself. It was my fault, I should have…" I start to break down, it's still so raw, and I've never actually said this out loud before, making it real. On a sob, I press on, "I should have…"

"Take your time, I'm listening. What is it that you think you should have done? Could have done?" Gone now the hard Dom, back is my tender lover, his words of encouragement murmured into my ear.

"I should have left him. Earlier. If I'd gone, left Kenny, David might not have died." My voice breaks as I force out the words, the terrible admission, the bitter truth I've held down, suppressed up until now.

Tom's tone is even, reasonable. "You can't know that. Babies *do* die. Sometimes, it's no one's fault. Not yours, not Kenny's."

At that I whirl on him, my thin veneer of control shattered. I scream at him, pounding his chest with my fists. "It *was* Kenny's fault. All his fault. And mine. He couldn't keep his fists to himself, always punching, always pushing me around. Wouldn't let me rest even though I was dog-tired all the time. And feeling so sick I just wanted to die. And always wanting sex even when he said I was fat and ugly. I hated him, hated him, but still I didn't leave. I should have left. I should have left..." I break down, my heaving sobs loud and gulping against his bare chest, the only sound in the silence of our room.

Tom tightens his arms around me, but as ever in my more emotional moments, he offers no comment, neither encouraging me to continue nor trying to stem my tears. He waits, caressing my back gently with his hands, soothing me with their firm, circular motion, holding me there until I'm ready. At last, my face still buried in his chest, I try to continue. It's slow, and it's painful, a wrenching, raw pain, the pain of loss and guilt and self-blame. And this time he makes no move to force eye contact, just lets me hide there, trembling, as I haltingly, hesitantly, tell him my story.

"I was pregnant. It was Kenny's baby too, but he didn't care, didn't want it. He just thought it was my problem, and a nuisance. As if I'd done it on purpose. Every time I was sick he complained. Or sneered. When I was tired he told me I was lazy, making excuses not to go to work. And we needed the money, my wages. He needed my money. I worked as a cleaner in an office block, most evenings, till late. I'd been at work that night we met you, when we, when we..."

"I know, love. It's all right. Don't worry about that now. Tell me about David."

"I never meant to get pregnant. It was at Christmas, he was drunk and he—and he... forced me. I was fighting, struggling, didn't make it easy so he just didn't bother with a condom. Just held me down and, and...and a few weeks later...well, I knew."

The pain and humiliation are as vivid now as they were then, the recollection enough to catapult me right back there into that grimy room, Kenny's drunken fumblings, his hands rough and hard, his breath tainted by beer, cigarettes and a two day old cold chicken biryani. I shudder, and Tom's gentle hands draw me once more into the here and now, urging me to continue my story.

"The day David died it was about a month after we—saw—you. I was six months pregnant, I'd had a cold, still had a cough—I felt rotten. I wanted to stay at home, stay in bed, miss work that day, but he wasn't having that. He dragged me out of bed around lunch time, sent me to the fish and chip shop for something for him to eat. When I got back I'd forgotten the salt and vinegar, and of course we had nothing like that in the house, so he was angry. Again. He punched me. Again. And this time I fell. I fell heavily, against the arm of the sofa, catching my 'bump'. It hurt. Straight away I knew I'd done some damage. Something was wrong. The sharp pain went dull, but didn't stop. Never went off. It was coming in waves like a cramp. I lay down on the sofa, on my side, hugging my bump, holding my baby close, as if I could protect him. I wanted to protect him. I even tried praying. Kenny just swore and carried on eating his chips, grumbling. I lay there, scared, hoping it might all die down, the pains might stop. They didn't, and when I went to the loo I was bleeding. I told Kenny, said I needed to go to the hospital. He said 'no', told me to go to bed if I had to. Even told me I could have a night off work after all. But I said I was okay, that I'd go to work later.

"Except I didn't. I had to wait, I waited in bed till it was time to go to my cleaning job, then I went out. Went straight to the hospital, and they admitted me. They did a scan, and that's when I knew it was all over. No heartbeat, my baby was dead. He'd been alive that morning, I'd felt him move. The doctor tried to explain, that the placenta had been dislodged, come unstuck, and that my baby had starved. It didn't take long, only a few hours. And I just thought, I've always thought, that if I'd gone to the hospital when it first happened, maybe, maybe they might have…done something. Anything. David might not have died. But by the time I could get away from Kenny, it was too late. By then no one could help."

I stop, crying silently now, drowning in the misery of that awful day, and waiting for Tom to point out the obvious, that I should have left Kenny weeks, months before it came to that. Or even defied him on that day, put my baby first.

Instead though, his response is soft, measured, reflective, "That bastard. Sweetheart, it wasn't your fault. None of it was your fault. It shouldn't have happened like that, but there was nothing you did wrong. You did all you could, as soon as you could. You have to believe that."

"I wish, I wish…"

"You did all you could. You loved your baby, I know that. You know it too."

I hesitate, but maybe I just needed to hear it from someone, someone I can trust. "I—yes. I still love him. I'll never forget him. Never." Then, a thought occurs suddenly. "His grave, it's here. In the cemetery in Gloucester. I've never been back, not since the day we buried him. Maybe I could…"

"We'll go. That's a good idea."

"My mother too, she's there as well."

"Your mother too. We'll go together. Visit them both."

I consider that possibility, reflecting sadly on the tragic events of nearly two years ago. I hadn't expected ever to go back to that cemetery in Gloucester, would not have wanted to. On my own, I doubt I ever could. But with Tom? Yes, with Tom it would be possible.

He waits, not intruding on my private thoughts, until I shift in his arms, my signal that I'm okay now.

Only then does he continue, "But there's more, isn't there? What about Kenny? Why's he so vindictive toward you now? I can see why you'd hate him, but what's his quarrel with you?"

I sigh, stiffen and shuffle around to huddle beside Tom on the bed, no longer hiding my face as I continue my story. "I hated him. Hated him for what he'd done, what he'd caused. I decided while I was still at the hospital that I was going to leave him. And when my mother turned up, offered me the chance to go home with her, I jumped at it, my escape route. I left the hospital in Bristol and came straight back here, with her. We planned David's funeral, just the two of us. And then the very next day, the day after we buried baby David, Kenny arrived, demanding that I go back to Bristol with him. He even threatened to kill Sadie—my mum's cat—if I didn't do what he wanted. I couldn't let that happen, couldn't let him hurt anyone else, so I packed my stuff and went back with him. Back to Bristol.

"But I hated him. Absolutely hated him. I couldn't bear the sight of him, couldn't bear him to even touch me. And he wanted sex. Said I'd been gone ages, and he had needs for Christ's sake!" I glance up, see Tom's face harden, his jaw clench, But for me, he smiles softly.

"Go on, love. What happened after you went back to Bristol?"

"I said I didn't want to, you know…"

He nods. "Yes, I know."

"I was still bleeding, from when David was born. He was disgusted—that's the only reason he didn't—force me again. But he didn't, not straight away, and so I had a bit of time. I wanted rid of him, had to get rid of him. I'd tried the obvious, tried just leaving, and he'd come after me and brought me back. Even though he knew I didn't want to come, didn't want to be with him anymore. And apart from my mum's I'd nowhere else to go. I felt trapped, scared, desperate to be on my own, anywhere away from him. So I needed to do something, anything to get rid of him." I glance back at Tom, willing him to understand.

His face is expressionless, he waits quietly.

I take a deep breath, hold his gaze as I confess what I did. "So, I turned him in."

Tom's mouth turns down, thoughtful, and he nods. Just once, his eyes never leaving mine. But it's enough to tell me he approves, accepts, understands why I did what I did.

"I phoned Crimestoppers, told them about Kenny and that he was part of some ram raiding that had been going on. They came and arrested him, questioned him. Then they let him go. Just let him go, can you believe it? I was past caring by then, at my wits' end, scared, desperate. I phoned Crimestoppers again, told them where the stuff from the raids was hidden. And at last, that was enough. His fingerprints were there, the evidence was clear. He got sent down, got three years for it."

I stop, watch Tom's face carefully for some reaction, some sign of how he's taking all this. He frowns, obviously something not adding up still.

"But, you went inside too. You lied for him, gave him an alibi. Why do that, if you wanted him in jail? Why lie for him? And why carry on lying even when it was clear he was guilty?"

I can explain this. "I was covering my tracks. Well, trying to. I thought, if I gave him an alibi, convinced him I was on his side, he'd never work out it was me who told the police. I was terrified of what he'd do if he found out." My voice drops to a whisper, *"When* he found out. He knows. He must know it was me. And that's why..."

At last, Tom leans back against the headboard, apparently satisfied. Or more or less so.

"Ram raiding? Not a solitary occupation, I'd guess? Were there others involved?"

I think about that. I suppose there must have been. "Yes, I guess. Probably. I never thought…"

"Could they have been some of those tossers we met today? Could there be more than just Kenny with a score to settle?"

The blood drains from my face, my heart skips as I finally realize the implications. I've been so fixated on Kenny, on avoiding him, on getting him out of my life, I never thought about the wider ramifications, the others involved in his criminal past. My past, now apparently catching up with me fast. Tom nods, looking thoughtful.

"Now it makes sense, explains why he was so mob-handed, why six big tough thugs would make the trip up here just for one skinny little girl." He grins at me. "No offense, love. They were all pissed off, and they all wanted a piece."

"Oh, God. They'll kill me. Won't they? They'll come back, next time you might not be there…"

"Nope. They're not gonna get the chance." Tom's voice is firm again, hard, confident. The Dom, once more in charge. "I somehow think, after today, most of them will have lost their enthusiasm. Kenny now, I suspect with him it could be more personal. But he might have had enough as well, who knows? In any case, I suggest we finish up what needs doing here, talk to your lawyer, the insurance, get the repairs to the house sorted out, visit the cemetery and then we head back up the M6 as soon as we can. And while we're here, you're never going to be on your own. There'll be me or Nathan with you, all the time. Preferably both of us. Speaking of which, we'll need to fill him in on all of this. He needs to know what he's up against, what's behind all this. Agreed?"

I nod absently as I look at him and wonder if it could be true. Can he — they — protect me? Would they? He's grabbed his phone from the low table beside the bed and he's punching in a text then fires it off to Nathan. Again, he catches my gaze, smiles his reassurance, his resolve as he stands up, ambles over to unlatch the door.

And I start to believe. I mouth the words — "Thank you." He strolls back to the bed, sits down and beckons me to him, and I go immediately. I wrap my arms tightly around his neck as he traces my collar bone with his lips.

"I wish, I just wish you'd told me all about all of this at the beginning. Why didn't you, Ashley?"

I think back to that crazy, confused time and the overwhelming emotion I felt then, the powerful driver that controlled everything I did in those early days and weeks at Smithy's Forge. "I was scared. Just plain scared I suppose. Scared of you, absolutely terrified of Nathan. After that first day, with you, it was — strange — but I didn't think you'd ever do anything worse to me than you had that day. I could cope with that. But Nathan — I was sure he was going to tell the police about me, and then I'd have gone back to jail. And — if that happened, I'd have still been inside when Kenny got out. He'd have been waiting for me. And I don't think I'd have ever managed to get away again..."

And there was something else I now realize, now recognize. It's personal, leaves me vulnerable, but I owe him an explanation. He's my Dom, I can't lie to him. "And I was lonely. Isolated. I couldn't go to Black Combe any more, couldn't talk to Rosie or Grace, I knew no one in the area except you. You were...my anchor. My visits to Greystones were the highlight of my week, my only chance to talk to anyone, the only human contact I had. I couldn't risk having you turn me away too. So I kept quiet about what had happened before. Our relationship was fragile, but it was all I had..."

With a groan he tips my face to his, kisses me. Then, "Christ, what a pair of absolute bastards we were, me and Nathan. When I think of what I did, how we treated you those first few weeks..."

"It doesn't matter now, it's done with." I'm kissing him back, wriggling closer as the towel slips to my waist and his hands cup my breasts. He flips me onto my back, leans in to take control.

"Bloody hell, you two, I'd suggest you get a room but..."

Shit! I never heard Nathan come in. Tom swears under his breath, turns his head to regard his friend sternly over his shoulder. "Don't you ever fucking knock?"

Nathan's grin is unrepentant as he settles himself in the one chair in the room, tips his half full glass at us cheerily. "Hell, bro, I was invited." He pulls his phone from his jeans pocket, makes a show of checking his texts again, then, "Yes, definite invitation there. So, are we planning a little ménage here? That's not our usual style of course, but if you insist I don't mind joining in, just by way of helping you out you understand..." He shakes his head, smiling at my shriek of embarrassed outrage.

I'm struggling under Tom's weight, trying desperately to make myself decent. Tom takes pity, raises himself slightly and tugs my towel back into place before rolling off. I can't help noticing his own towel has borne up far better than mine.

"Shit, you pick your moments." He settles himself on the bed, propped up against the headboard and motions for me to join him there.

I do, and he casually drops an arm across my shoulders, indicating his support, his solidarity. And I appreciate it, I definitely do.

"Okay, we needed a word with you. Ashley's been telling me what all this stuff with Kenny's all about, and we agreed you need to be in the picture too. Okay, Ashley?"

I nod reluctantly. I can see why we need to tell him but still. Buoyed up—if only slightly—by Tom's support I look Nathan in the eye, his face now serious as he waits to hear what we—I—have to say. I start with my customary apology.

"I feel so embarrassed by all this. It just confirms what you said, when I first arrived at Smithy's Forge. I've brought you trouble, just like you said I would. I'm sorry…"

Tom stiffens, starts to protest, to reassure me yet again, but it's Nathan's hand that's raised, silencing us both.

"I know, I know all that, know exactly what you're going to say. Heard it all before, too many times. So understand this, Ms McAllister, because I don't want to have to repeat myself. If I hear one more word from you about being sorry, about bringing trouble our way, about being a burden or any more of that fucking crap, I'll be holding Tom's jacket while he puts you over his knee and spanks you. Then I'll take over and spank you myself. And believe me, neither one of us is going to be gentle. So enough now. We care about you. We all care about you, and we've all done things we're not proud of. Let's move on. Please."

He's glaring at me, and the room's silent. I gaze at him, wide-eyed, wait for Tom's reaction. When it comes, it's in the form of one of his customary low chuckles. "Does that seem clear enough love? Either you drop the apologizing or you drop that towel and bend over. You choose."

It's certainly a tantalizing image, but I know my limitations. One angry Dom is more than enough for me. My answer is quiet, but firm as I look from one to the other, "I'll keep the towel, if that's all right with both of you."

"Good answer. Now please continue." Nathan settles back to listen.

I open my mouth to start, then close it again. Take a deep breath, try once more to work out where to start.

Tom grips my shoulder. "Would you like me to tell him, you just chip in if I get anything wrong, or miss anything important?"

I nod gratefully. "Yes please."

"Okay, this goes back to when Ashley's baby died..." Tom calmly, concisely, accurately, tells Nathan what happened, how I came to leave Kenny, how he came to be arrested, and my own stay at Her Majesty's pleasure. Nathan's eyebrows shoot up at that, although if I didn't know better I'd have thought he looked vaguely impressed. He definitely looks impressed as Tom explains about my calls to Crimestoppers. On hearing that again, another thought strikes me. "Should we tell the police about this last stuff? We should, shouldn't we? If he set the fire, I mean... Or is that just me grassing again?"

Nathan and Tom exchange a look, then Tom speaks for them both. "It's all of us being honest, law-abiding citizens. And, sweetheart, this is serious stuff your Kenny's got himself into now. Arson, attempted murder, probably attempted abduction too. We'll definitely tell the police what we think. It's up to them to prove it. And just assuming they manage to string a few clues together and come up with the right arsonist this time, he'll only be getting what he deserves. It's not your responsibility to protect him. He ought to pay for what he's done. Especially to you. Maybe this time they'll lock him up for a bit longer."

That had occurred to me too. "He was sentenced to three years, but he can't have served more than eighteen months for the ram raids if he's already out."

Nathan nods. "Makes your four months look even more outrageous, given what others seem to get away with."

I shudder. "And, I really thought I'd be going back. Today. If it hadn't been for Julia Montgomery…" I look up at him again. "It was kind of you to get me a lawyer."

"Me? Not guilty, Ms McAllister. That was Tom. Eva gave the detailed instructions because we were both in the car on the way down here, we kept losing signal. But it was Tom who remembered that Jules was down in this part of the country visiting someone or other."

"Yeah," Tom agrees, "she mentioned her old school reunion last week. I was chatting to her at The Hermitage. You were at the loo I think, love."

I look from one to the other, baffled. "But I thought… Julia Montgomery said her firm was retained by Darke Associates. That's your company. Your corporate lawyers…"

Nathan smiles widely. "*Our* company. *Our* corporate lawyers. Who do you think's the 'associate' part. Tom owns fifty percent. I started the company, and then Tom came on board. We just never bothered to change the name. I tend to lead on the regeneration stuff, construction projects, development. Tom leads on rural enterprises, renewable energy, that sort of thing. We each have a few other interests outside the company, small things really, but the bulk of our business activity is a fifty-fifty partnership. I'm the one who always gets rolled out in a suit, and yes, I tend to deal with the lawyers, but golden boy here's the creative genius" He glances sharply at Tom. "You should have told her all this, bro."

Tom shrugs. "Never came up. 'Till now. And if we're all quite done airing our little secrets, unless you intend to stay and watch, I'd like you to bugger off now. I'm about to fuck my sub until she screams and I don't intend to share."

Straight faced, Nathan gets to his feet, downs the remainder of his drink then nods politely to me. He turns to Tom. "Now that's downright unsociable, but hey, I'll leave you two to work up an appetite. I suppose I could always phone Eva and talk dirty with her — usually gets me my reward in the end. So, I'll see you in the restaurant. Will an hour be enough time?"

Grinning, Tom turns to me, hunched up on the bed, my face burning, mortified at their casual exchange. "What do you think, Ashley, can I make you scream in an hour? You were saying you wanted a decent fuck, and I did promise you a spanking too. Will that be enough time for you? I wouldn't want you to feel — hurried." He waits a moment, then, "Ashley? An hour?"

My mind rapidly becoming a blank I mumble my response. "I, yes, yes — that should be fine. Thank you." The door closes behind Nathan with a soft click, an instant before I'm grabbed and flipped onto my stomach, the towel sailing through the air.

Chapter Nine

As I snuggle up in bed next to Tom, the crisp white hotel sheets cool against my naked skin, I'm reflecting drowsily on what a bizarre day it has been. It started so normally with breakfast at Black Combe and ended here in Gloucester, stopping off at my mother's fire-damaged house and custody suite at the local police station in between. I'm still deeply thankful not to be spending my first night back in prison. But for Tom, and Julia…

Our evening meal in the hotel restaurant was a surprisingly convivial affair, given that my bottom was smarting from the attention it had received only an hour earlier, and I could only sit still for a few minutes at a time. Both men had knowing smirks on their faces, and Tom kindly offered to fetch me a pillow from the room to sit on. So considerate. I thanked him politely but declined, glowering at him.

We planned what we needed to do, all three of us in agreement that the sooner we could get out of Gloucester and back to Yorkshire the better. Our first hurdle was to tell the police what had happened after

I'd been released from their tender clutches, hopefully set them on the right track. I dreaded that, convinced they'd manage to find some reason to point the finger at me again, but in fact it went well. PC Tall and Stupid was no doubt off duty by the time Tom phoned the police station and asked to speak to someone in connection with the arson attack. As luck would have it, the young sergeant who came to see us at the hotel was sharp and polite and seemed to grasp entirely the significance of Kenny's presence in Gloucester. Nathan had also noted the registration number of the van so, unless it's stolen, it's only a matter of time before the police start to round up my would-be abductors.

After the police sergeant left, we considered our next moves over coffee in the hotel bar. We agreed to be at the offices of Hampson and Miller in time for them opening at nine o'clock in the morning, and from there we can instruct my friend Mr Miller regarding insurance, arranging the repairs, and so on. That just leaves the cemetery, a visit I'm anticipating with a mixture of dread and joy. But mostly joy. I really do believe this could be a chance, a real chance, at closure. My opportunity to move on, to really move on this time.

Nathan was the first to head back upstairs to his room, I suspect for a late-night telephone conversation with Eva. Tom and I were not far behind. And we're all agreed, we definitely don't want to stay another night in Gloucester if we can help it.

* * * *

The meeting with Mr Miller went incredibly smoothly. He was visibly shocked at the attitude of the police, shaking his head at the idiocy of the whole idea. "Pity they didn't interview me before leaping to conclusions. Anyone with a commercial head could have told them this was no insurance scam. That house is a sound investment, turning a respectable profit. Very respectable indeed. It would make no financial sense at all for Miss McAllister to destroy her business." More head shaking, more disgruntled muttering, then down to business. Given that the police have now been disabused of their foolish notions regarding my part in this whole affair, he assured us that there would be no barrier to submitting the insurance claim on the basis that the fire was started deliberately, by persons unknown. Well, persons not yet proven — I'm pretty certain who did it even if I'm at something of a loss as to exactly why. Mr Miller was happy to arrange for estimates for the repairs, complete the insurance forms and to oversee the works in due course, consulting or reporting to me as required. We left his office knowing the matter was now in safe hands.

Our next, and final, stop is the cemetery. We cruise up the central driveway in Nathan's Porsche, my own car waiting for us back at the hotel. Huge imposing gravestones tower over us on both sides as I direct Nathan first to the small, discreet plot where my mother was buried a little over a year ago. Nathan parks the car nearby and we all three walk in silence to the graveside, the small headstone announcing the presence there of Susan Spencer —

1970 – 2012
A much loved mother, sadly missed.

I'm thinking that maybe I should commission something grander, something more in keeping with the wonderful woman she was. Dry-eyed, I reflect on a life cut cruelly short, and I wish she could have seen me now, enjoying the future we planned together and expected to share. I particularly wish that she could meet Tom, that she could hear all about my thriving new business, visit me in my new home, meet my friends.

But it's not to be. I'll always miss her, but her legacy is me, and the life I now have, in a large part due to her. I thank her silently, philosophically, and feel I'm at last ready to move on.

This next visit is much, much harder for me. Much more painful. The loss of my mother was devastating, but I know I survived it intact. The loss of my child, though, killed a part of me, too. Part of me is buried here under this cold earth, and I'll never again feel quite whole without him. Tom and Nathan stand quietly back, flanking me a few yards behind as I stumble forward to the plot in the stillborn babies' garden where David is actually buried. Tears stream unchecked as I recall that dreadful day when my mother and I stood here and watched as David's tiny, tiny coffin was lowered into the ground. I think of what might have been, what he might have become, what he might have achieved. He'd have been around eighteen months old by now, a toddler probably. I wonder what he'd have looked like. Would he have taken after me? Or—God forbid—Kenny? I think about what my life might have been like but for this tragedy. If David hadn't died I might well have still been with Kenny now, struggling to bring up my child, maybe even pregnant again, God help me. God help all of us.

I shudder, not yet ready to think in terms of silver linings, but I do thank whoever might be out there listening for my second chances. And maybe I'll have a second chance at motherhood, maybe it could be different the next time. I look over my shoulder, my gaze still watery, and I see Tom a few yards away, silent, patient. He smiles briefly, his head cocked to one side, asking permission. I answer by holding out my hand and he comes to me, takes my hand then he folds his arms around me and just holds me.

I hear the crunch of gravel as Nathan walks away to wait for us in the car.

* * * *

As we walk back into the farmhouse that first day back, Tom slams the door shut then shoves me up against it, promising me a decent fuck in some privacy at last. I respond along the lines of preferring something rather more on the indecent side, and with a knowing smile, loaded with wicked intent, Tom calls my bluff. I should have known better. He walks over to the fridge, grabs a couple of cold Pepsis then takes my hand to tow me up the stairs behind him. He leads me into our bedroom and instructs me to undress. Fast.

I do as I'm told, quickly shedding my jeans, hip length tunic top and underwear, all the time watching Tom out of the corner of my eye. He glances at me, his warning clear. I know the rules and I drop my gaze, stand perfectly still, looking at the floor. I hear as Tom reaches under the bed, draws out one of the 'toys' he keeps there. Out of the corner of my eye I see it is the spreader bar. He turns to me, and with a brief flick of his head indicates I'm to get onto the bed. I do as he's asked, but turn to look at him over my shoulder. He stops, one eyebrow raised in query.

"I'd like to ask you something, if that's allowed. Just now, I mean."

I detect a flash of irritation, then it's gone. "Is it important?"

"Yes. To me it is."

"Very well then. And would you prefer to turn around, and face me while you talk?"

"I would. Thank you."

He nods, and still kneeling, I turn. He doesn't approach me, continues to stand, towering over me, waiting. I place my hands on my knees and drop my gaze to them.

"I thought we agreed you could face me. Look up, Ashley. Look at me. And tell me what's on your mind."

I lift my gaze, and without preamble tell him what I want. "I want another baby. I want to try again."

He has the presence of mind not to register surprise if that's his reaction. Or maybe it isn't. Those long minutes earlier today, spent beside David's grave together, convinced me that I could re-write my future, choose a different course. Maybe he felt it too. In any case, now he simply nods.

"I expected that. Not quite so soon, perhaps, but I did expect it. Are you sure?"

"Yes, I am sure. This is what I want. This is how I can put it right, regain control…"

"Control? A strange choice of word, especially just at this moment."

"I mean, control of my life, my future. That's okay, isn't it? I mean, you've never said…"

He raises his hand to silence me, smiles at me. "Yes, you do control what happens to you. Always. Even here. Nothing happens that you don't want, that you don't agree to. You know that. And if a baby is truly what you want, then as far as I'm concerned you can have that too."

"Really? You mean it? I can stop taking the pill and, and see what happens."

He smiles wryly. "Well, I think we both know what's likely to happen, but yes. You can if you want to. It's your choice. Always your choice, Ashley."

I start forward, intending to throw my arms around him, but he stops me with one of his imperious Dom gestures and I subside back onto my knees, my eyes downcast although inside I'm singing. And he knows it.

"Are we done talking for now? Can we continue?"

"Yes. Yes, Sir."

"Excellent. Then please turn around."

Again, I turn away from him and wait.

"Lean forward please, put your hands on the bed in front of you." His instruction is delivered in his soft Dom tone, firm, commanding, but infinitely courteous.

I do as he's asked, and he steps forward, placing his palm on my bottom to gently caress each globe there before sliding his hand down the back of my left leg. Reaching my heel, he gently slides his hand underneath, lifts my foot to slip the ankle strap from one end of the spreader bar onto my left ankle. He tightens it, sliding his fingers under it to make sure it's secure but not uncomfortable. He then repeats the action with my right ankle.

"I'm going to push your ankles apart now. Don't try to resist, you'll end up with unpleasant bruises, just open your legs wide and support yourself on your hands. Okay?"

"Yes, Sir." I place my weight on my arms as he pulls my ankles wide apart, the spreader bar opening between them. At last—satisfied he has me positioned to his liking—he stops and locks the bar in place. I push myself up on my hands, turn to look at him over my shoulder. "Is this a spanking position?"

"Could be. Not this time though. This time, it's your arse I'm interested in. Give me your hands, the right one first please."

Puzzled, I reach back, unsteady now as I try to balance on my widely spread knees and just my left hand. He takes my hand and quickly secures my wrist to my right ankle. "Now your other hand." The outcome now obvious, I let him position my left hand and secure it to my ankle, forcing my weight forward. I turn my head, my cheek flat on the bed, my shoulders now taking my weight. My bottom is in the air, my thighs spread wide, offering a perfect view. Tom straightens, stands back to admire me from the foot of the bed.

"Looking so good, Ashley, so damned good. I love you so smooth, so truly naked. Are you comfortable?"

"I—not exactly."

"Oh, dear, sorry about that. This better?" And he slips one long finger inside me, fast, hard, deep. I cry out, and he immediately withdraws it. "Better with, or without? Which do you prefer, Ashley?"

I gasp, clench around the emptiness inside me, then respond, "With. It's better with."

"Then say 'please'."

"Please. Please…"

"Please what?"

"Please, Sir." I grind out the words, my body desperate now for some contact, for friction, for anything. I can feel the wetness gathering, flowing freely now as my anticipation mounts, my clit and pussy quivering, aching to be touched again as he makes me wait. Makes me beg.

"You're very wet, Ashley. Tell me, what makes you wetter? This, or this?" He plunges two fingers inside me, at the same time as he reaches under me with his other hand to flick my clitoris. "Which do you like best?"

I groan, desperate to move, to raise myself up farther, press against him, but I'm completely immobilized, helpless. His fingers are still inside me, but unmoving now. I squeeze around them, clenching.

"Ah, baby, that feels good. I want you to do that to my cock soon. Will, you do that, if I put my cock inside you will you squeeze me like that?"

"Yes, yes, anything. I just, please, I need you to…"

"This? Is this what you need? What you want?" And at last his fingers are moving, sliding in and out of me, thrusting, exploring, probing. He angles them to hit my inner pleasure spot, stroking it, pressing on it.

I scream, stiffen under his hands. Again he reaches for my clit, this time tracing his fingertip lightly along its length, front to back. I'm gasping now, moaning, rocking as I try desperately to achieve the release I need. My climax starts to build, I feel it surging deep within me, my senses all coalescing on that spot where he's exploring me with his fingers, stroking, pressing hard. I start to shake, to stiffen ready for the inner pyrotechnics just moments away now. And he stops. Again he stops. I'm almost crying now, my frustration painful, unbearable. I'm swearing under my breath, always dangerous around Tom in Dom mode and this is no exception. He slaps my bottom hard, once, twice, three times.

"Be polite, Ashley. Now, we've got you warmed up a little, so it's time for some proper fun." There's a faint squelch of lube as he squirts it onto his fingers, then directly onto me, onto my anus beautifully displayed and positioned for him. He doesn't speak, doesn't need to as his intentions are perfectly clear. Even so, I gasp as he penetrates me with his finger, gently but firmly circling to open the sphincter. Quickly he works a second finger inside me, and I groan as he presses deeper.

"Am I hurting you? I'm doing this quickly today. You do seem to be opening nicely, but I can slow down." His fingers are inside me, but he stops, waits for me to respond.

And I do. "No, I'm fine."

So he continues. His firm, thrusting movements make short work of any further muscular resistance, and soon three well lubricated fingers are thrust fully inside my anus. Holding them there, and using them to keep me in position, he again reaches for my pussy, finger fucking me mercilessly until I'm on the point of climax once more. And this time I'm not surprised when he stops a fraction short of the mark. I'm frustrated, desperate, ready to weep, to beg, to promise anything if he'll only let me come. But not surprised. Pulling his fingers from my pussy but continuing to possess my bum, he leans over me, lifts the hair from my face.

"Look at me, Ashley. Tell me what you want me to do to you." His voice is quiet, soft and low and seductive. I open my eyes, and he holds my gaze, smiling, knowing. "Do you want me to let you come now?"

"Yes. Please. Please, Sir..." I can hear my ragged breath, the catch in my voice.

"And what if I say no? What if I decide you haven't earned an orgasm? What then? Maybe I should let you wait a little longer, you'd appreciate it all the more."

"No, please don't. Please, Tom, Sir, I need you to— Please make me come now. I can't bear this..."

He smiles at me as he nods, the expression warm and sensual. "Okay then, lovely Ashley. As you've asked me so nicely. I'm going to let you come, then I'm going to fuck you. Here." He jerks his fingers in my anus to make sure I'm under no illusions about what's coming.

I close my eyes again, wait for him to make good on his promise. And this time I don't have to wait long. He trails his clever fingers once more along my clitoris, but this time pressing firmly, rubbing harder as I start to writhe and moan, as the orgasm fluttering just below the surface surges forward, past the point of no return, and continuing to work me as I convulse and clench and scream as the sensation overwhelms me. Wave after glorious, delicious wave of sensual delight washes over me, through me, starting at my quivering core and rushing outwards, then back again as he draws every last tingle of my response from me, wrings every last gasp and moan from my throat. At last, it's done. At last I start to calm again, to regain my senses. I'm boneless, my muscles useless. I'd collapse fully onto the bed but I'm held in place, unable to move a muscle.

Wordlessly, Tom takes his time sliding his fingers out of me. There's a snap of latex as he slips a condom on before I feel his hands on my hips and the head of his cock slipping just inside my anus. Easily, slick, he's obviously smeared lube over the condom too to insure an easy entry. I'm grateful for that as he presses home, slides fully into my unresisting body.

"Christ, baby, that feels so good." He pulls back, right out of me, then repeats the process again. And again.

Each time he withdraws fully, just for the sheer joy of entering me again. And each time he's faster, plunging harder, deeper, until I cry out. Then he stops, it's enough, and he thrusts more gently, takes his time, the friction building as he uses me, plays with me, enjoys me. Then he leans forward, his fingers once more at my clit, this time the familiar rolling and tugging. It's good, gloriously good, and I make a soft purring in my throat, the only sound I'm capable of. Again, my climax starts to build, but this time he urges me on, his words of encouragement heightening my wild, wicked pleasure.

I come again, less violently this time, but every sensation exquisitely teased from me. And he's there, with me. Tom gives a muttered curse, the pressure within me increasing as his thrusts gather strength, and the final deep, stiff plunge as he holds me still and finally he ejaculates deep inside me.

He pulls out immediately, and I wait, expecting to be released from the spreader bar, to at last be allowed to collapse onto the bed and sleep. Instead he gets off the bed and walks across the room. Exhausted, I force myself to prize my eyes open. I see him dispose of the condom in the bin, and note idly that somehow, incredibly, he's still fully dressed in his jeans and white T-shirt. He picks something up from the dressing table, comes back toward me, sees me watching him. He holds the object up between his thumb and forefinger. A butt plug. A big one. I moan, surely he can't…I can't.

Seemingly he can. And so can I. He uses his left hand to ease the cheeks of my bum apart and the other to slip the butt plug inside my anus. It *is* big. And it's fucking cold. I shriek and earn myself a swift, hard slap.

"No rude words, Ashley. I've warned you. Swear at me again and I'll put more stripes on this lovely arse of yours. Is that clear?"

My bottom smarting, my back passage shriveling around the icy intruder, I'm almost sobbing.

"Is that clear, Ashley?" Another hard slap.

I force myself to answer. "Yes. But it's cold."

"Mmm, not long out of the freezer. I remembered how much you liked the ice lolly trick. Are you swearing at me again?"

I'm sobbing now, gulping in air, shaking. I answer him desperately, "No! No, I'm not. I promise. Please, I don't want you to hit me."

He hesitates, leans in close. "Ashley, are you safe wording?"

"No. Yes. Yes. Amber. It's amber..." I'm sobbing, oddly hurt and humiliated, exposed, vulnerable and wishing he'd just be nice to me.

His palm is on my bum again, but soft this time, a soft caress. He calms me by his gentle touch, his quiet, tender words. "I'll take it out, if that's what you want. But if you can stick with it, it will be good. I'll make it feel good, for you. I promise. And no more spanking, at least not tonight. No matter how rude you are. Deal?"

"Yes. Deal. Thank you."

"You're welcome. You can safe word any time you like. Remember that, Ashley. Okay, so no spanking, but what *do* you want? This maybe?" He slides his fingers inside my pussy once more, gentle, soothing, warm in contrast to the frigid presence in my anus.

I shiver, the clash of sensations overwhelming my senses, confusing me, stimulating me wildly.

"Is this okay?"

"Yes, yes, that's... Oh, yes."

He pleasures me lazily, readying me again before he stands, swiftly peels off his jeans and T-shirt then comes to kneel behind me. "I think a nice, hard fuck now. That suit you?"

Beyond words I mumble something incoherent, but he assumes it to be agreement. Leaning over me now on all fours, he slips his cock into me. It's wonderful, absolutely wonderful. I moan, and remember his instructions of much earlier, that I should squeeze him. I clench my inner muscles, deliberately convulsing, seizing him, holding him, caressing him with my body in the only way I can. He holds my hips, sliding his palms up my sides to cup the undersides of my breasts. I savor every stretch and scrape of flesh on flesh, his hardness stretching and filling me.

Almost spent, the pleasure builds by degrees this time, but builds nevertheless. Tom's moans of appreciation tell me that the feeling is mutual. The intensity of the cold inside me soon dissipates and the exquisitely gentle pressure inside me takes over, increasing the sense of fullness and heightening the pleasure of every stroke. This is slow, comfortable fucking, sweet, gentle and achingly tender. Despite my restraints I arch under my Dom, totally his, purring once more as my pleasure washes me, warms me, wraps around me.

My orgasm, when it finally comes, takes me softly, smoothly, tumbling me into the feather bed of shared sensuality as we surrender together. The warm wash of Tom's semen splashes across my cervix then fills my pussy, adding to the pools of moisture already coating me. He slows, and finally he's unmoving inside me. He leans forward to kiss my neck before gently withdrawing. He swiftly unfastens my restraints, first my wrists then my ankles, and I at last collapse in a tangle of aching limbs. I hear the thud of the spreader hitting the floor, then Tom lifts me, tugging the duvet back to ease me underneath it. He pulls the quilt up to my chin, crouching beside the bed to nuzzle my nose with his.

"I need to talk to you, now, while it's fresh in your mind. While you can remember just how you felt. Are you okay? Was I too rough with you there? You said you didn't want me to hit you…"

I open my eyes, smile at him. "It was good. Really. I'm fine."

"Ashley? Tell me."

I open my eyes again, force myself to concentrate. This is important. "It's nothing. I like it when you, when you—spank me. Really. Most of the time. It's just that, sometimes, I need you to just—be kind to me. But I can't always ask, can't always say exactly how I'm feeling when you're… When we…"

"You *can* tell me, that's what safe words are for. And eventually you did, but not before you'd become upset, scared. You're my submissive, so it's my job to know. To listen. And to know when 'no, don't' means just that. Safe words are fool proof though. As soon as you said 'amber' I knew what you needed. Next time you feel like that, please, tell me earlier." He nuzzles my nose again, kisses my lips lightly. "So, are we okay, love?"

I close my eyes again, almost asleep now, and mutter my final words to him on this subject. "Yes. Always."

Chapter Ten

The morning after he introduced me to the highs and lows of the spreader bar, Tom rustles up our customary bacon sandwiches and coffee, and settles himself across from me at the kitchen table. We're both chewing quietly, planning the day ahead, when he fixes me with a look—that look of his that signals something serious coming my way. I know what it's likely to be.

"So, we're to be parents then, you and me? That's the plan, right?"

I look at him, holding his gaze, suddenly filled with doubt, hesitancy and fear that his agreement last night might have been just intended to keep me happy, acquiescent. I do him an injustice.

"Yes. That's right. You said it was okay…"

"It is. It's a lovely idea. Count me in." He grins, and it's infectious.

My smile must be positively radiant as I glow back at him. A baby. My own baby. Safe, well, healthy. And most important of all—alive. It could happen. It really could happen.

"But we need to talk, there are conditions, things we need to have settled." Tom's tone is serious despite his warm smile.

"What? What conditions?" My optimism evaporates as I watch his face take on just a hint of his Dom sternness, his solemn green gaze holding my now slightly desperate one.

"Number one, should I be talking to your father? Should I be asking his permission to marry you?"

Now this I hadn't expected. Never considered this possibility. I blurt out my surprise, blunt to the point of rudeness, "No! Of course not. Why should you...? I mean, I don't want, don't expect... There's no need to marry me."

Apparently less offended than he might be, he just grins at me. "Ah, my generous offer not an answer to a maiden's prayer then? Okay, set that idea to one side. We may need to re-visit it later, but for now, let's look at the most pressing stuff."

I'm finding this whole discussion little short of bewildering—I've no experience of this sort of conversation, this sort of planning. My confusion must be written all over my face.

"Don't look so worried, love, I told you I'd keep you safe. And the baby. Our baby. I'd want to look after you in any case, but it's particularly important to us, isn't it? You know why."

I nod, gratitude and relief flooding me as I wait for whatever's coming next.

"Given our—lifestyle—I'll need to know as soon as you suspect you may be pregnant. You understand why, don't you? The early weeks are the most fragile, we'll need to look after you, wrap you in cotton wool, so to speak. And definitely no roughing you up. That means no spanking, no whipping, no caning. Nothing remotely…" He's obviously searching for the right word.

Keen to help, I put in my suggestion, "Brutal."

He fixes me with a stern look, his Dom persona surfacing. "I prefer 'physically challenging'. Demanding perhaps…"

I nod meekly, the perfect submissive. "As you say. Sir."

"Sassy little wench. You're not pregnant yet, so have a care. Seriously though, you'll tell me? Yes?"

"Yes. I promise. Do nipple clamps count as brutal? Sorry, I mean demanding?"

He scowls at me, rocking his hand to indicate 'could be'.

"I see. And clit clips?"

He shakes his head. "Depends, but probably not."

"Butt plugs?"

He laughs, shaking his head. "For the avoidance of doubt, sex toys are fine. I think I read somewhere that orgasms are very healthy for pregnant women. Probably help with conception too. We'll have to put in even more effort."

More effort. *More* orgasms! I feel my face flush at that prospect, but manage to offer a suitably restrained response.

"Thank you, Sir. I appreciate your help and your concern." Then, "What about The Hermitage? Can we still go there?" We've become fairly frequent visitors to the kinky club in Leeds, although our activities are mainly confined to the private rooms and the health spa.

He considers that briefly. "Fine, but as a spectator sport." He regards me seriously, his eyes narrowed in thought. "Not sure how well your corset would fit, obviously, might need to buy you a maternity one. I wonder if they sell anything like that at Marks and Spencer?" He grins at me. "What about your business? You're just beginning to get somewhere. You'd need to take some time out, at least for a few months."

"I know, but I think it could work. I work from home, and I can do my editing and such like when you're here to look after the baby. If that's okay with you, I mean. I don't expect you to do a lot of baby-sitting..."

He holds up a hand to stop my flow. "Ashley, I'll help. You don't have to ask. And I won't be doing any baby-sitting. Baby-sitting's what you do for other people's children. With your own it's called parenting. If we do this, we do it together. But it'll affect you the most and I'm just thinking it might be difficult. For you."

"I think I'll be fine. Tom—I want to do this. I really do."

He smiles at me, his gaze tender, affectionate. And caring. "I know. I've seen you with Isabella. I *do* know."

"And, I could probably pay for a child minder if I needed one, later on. And perhaps me and Eva could help each other out. I'll ask her..."

"Parenting, remember. We'll share the childcare. And the costs." He sips his coffee idly, his gaze still holding me. Then, "You've obviously given this a lot of thought, Ashley."

I nod. "I have. It's what I want, what I need."

His mouth turns down, calm, philosophical, obviously accepting my resolve to do this thing that's going to turn our lives upside down. "I can see that. So, let's make it happen."

Stern Dom or not, I leap to my feet and run around the table to plant myself on his lap and huge kiss on his mouth. "Thank you, thank you, thank you. I love you. God, I love you…"

He raises his head, captures my face between his palms. "The feeling's mutual, Ashley."

And I'm kissing him again.

* * * *

Back at Greystones, daily life resumes. Reinvigorated, my eye once more firmly fixed on a future I can see unfolding for myself, a future I can strive for and is now within reach, I throw myself even more energetically into my new life, incredibly thankful to have this chance. To *still* have this chance. I'll probably never know for sure what Kenny and his bunch of thugs intended to do to me that day in Gloucester when they all turned up at my mother's house, but deep down I do suspect they might have killed me. Or Kenny might have.

Tom and Nathan play it down, but I'm pretty sure they saved my life that day. Attacking me, abducting me even, would have been an ill-fated, senseless thing to do and Kenny would never have gotten away with it, but he's too stupid, too deluded, too obsessed with his own self-importance to ever realize that. And in any case, no matter how heavily the full weight of the law might eventually fall once more upon Kenny's dim-witted head, none of that would have helped me much. The best I could have hoped for would have been that someone would have had the sense to bury me with my mother and baby, but that would be cold comfort indeed—for me, and for those around me who care.

For the first few weeks after we arrived back I was nervous, although I prefer to think of it as natural caution. I tended to stay close to the farm, only going out with Tom, or maybe just scuttling across to Black Combe in my car to spend time with Grace, or Eva and her mother, Victoria, who seems to have been permanently installed in Nathan's spare bedroom.

Rosie's animated chatter is delightful as always, distracting and amusing, but I have to confess somewhat mixed feelings about baby Isabella. She's lovely, an impossibly pretty little baby, sweet natured as well. Eva is incredibly lucky—I know that better than most. From the beginning, Isabella's sparkling presence has reminded me of my own loss, and for that reason I should probably avoid her. It wouldn't be difficult, no one forces me to pick her up, to cuddle her at every opportunity. No one insists that I volunteer to give her a bottle every time she gurgles or whimpers. No one expects me to be the first to reach for the Pampers when it's time to change her nappy. But no one stops me either, and I silently bless Eva, Nathan and Grace—and Victoria too—for their tolerance and quiet understanding.

Perhaps sensing my need for him, Tom's been around the farm a lot, much more than usual. He's very busy just now, gearing up for the music festival in a few weeks' time. The place is over-run with contractors and suppliers, a hive of activity. But despite the manic frenzy surrounding us much of the time, Tom's always happy to spend time with me. We talk—a lot—and the sex between us has been off the scale during these last weeks of the summer.

The encounter in Gloucester was terrifying, unnerving, but gradually I'm starting to relax again, to regain my confidence, my self-belief. With Barney in tow most days I'm once more enjoying my trips up onto the moors I now think of as my own, bouncing across the rugged landscape on my beloved quad bike, invariably making long detours to avoid the stiles and narrow footpaths that hikers seem so fond of. There was no direct evidence linking Kenny to the arson attack, so the police questioned him but then had to let him go. The case remains open, but meanwhile the insurance company has settled my claim, paid up and the repairs are well underway. The damage was limited mostly to the ground floor so the house should be fit to let to students again by the time the new academic year starts in October. Mr Miller reports to me regularly, usually about once a week, and I'm intrigued to find myself doing the arithmetic to work out how much loss of income I should be anticipating and the impact of this on my long-term business plan. The financial losses are not that great, and I'm once more intrigued. When did I become such a capitalist?

And speaking of which, conscious I've neglected my business with all these other distractions, I made arrangements for another trip to the Peak District. I spent four glorious days photographing the High Peak landscape, bathed in late summer sunshine, glowing with oranges, golds and vivid greens. I renewed my business contacts in Bakewell and Tideswell, and found a couple of more potential outlets. So many tourist hubs here, and I'm fast beginning to realize the potential of the many and various local markets, galas and shows. I'm pondering a series of prints themed around food — producing, growing, selling, eating — something for everyone. I could call it The Food Chain.

My head brimming with possibilities, I mulled over the prospects in the Yorkshire Dales, as I made my way back up the M1. Back home. Back to Tom.

*** *

Barn. Now.

Why? Is there a problem?

What part of NOW is not clear?

Ah, like that is it? Who'd have thought he could inject that Dom tone into a text? But he has, and I know I need to be on my way.

It's been raining. Again. That makes three days on the trot when I've been unable to get out onto the moors. I've been catching up on my edits and Photoshopping, but there's a limit to that, even for me. I've got a whole new batch of Peak District material ready to send to my printer, and a lot more stuff in the pipeline now. I could start on the Lakes soon. If it ever stops raining.

Right now I'm in need of some serious diversionary therapy. And it appears my Dom has something in mind. Bring it on.

I shut down my computer, careful to save all my work in progress. I may be randy as hell and on a promise, but I'm not stupid. A few minutes later I'm wrestling the huge barn door open, just enough for me to slip through into the gloomy interior.

I stand just inside the door, looking for Tom, listening. The place is silent, eerily so. But he's here, here somewhere. Even if it wasn't for his text I'd know. I can feel his eyes on me. I shiver, the involuntary shudder creeping down my spine like ice. I'm not comfortable, I wish he'd show himself.

"Tom, Tom, where are you?" I call out, my voice echoing around the cavernous, dusty space, bouncing back at me from the bales of hay and unused farm implements. I turn, looking all around, and up into the open loft above my head. He must be up there.

I start for the ladder and shriek loudly as a hand lands on my shoulder.

"Where do you think you're going?" Tom's voice, deep, low, right against my ear.

"Christ, you scared the shit out of me! What do you think you're doing, creeping up on me like that? Where the hell did you spring from?" Dom or not, I can't keep the anger from my voice, an anger born of nervousness. He really creeped me out.

"That's no way to talk to your Master, little Ashley. Maybe you'd like to apologize. Now, before I really get irritated with you. You wouldn't like me to get irritated, would you? Remember the last time I had cause to discipline you in here?"

"I don't bloody care. You nearly gave me a heart attack. I…"

My tirade is rudely interrupted by a hand over my mouth, and Tom's voice is in my ear, hard now, his warning tone unmistakable, "I'm sorry I scared you, I didn't mean to. But you got my text, you knew I was here. And now, you've said enough. Too much. You badly need a little refresher course in respect, I think. I've obviously been much too lenient with you recently. You've been getting too much gentle fucking and clit clips, and not enough discipline. That changes, here, now."

He drops his hand from my mouth to cup my chin, holding my head up, pressed against his unrelenting chest. "Do you agree, Ashley? Do you think you need discipline too?"

The threat is there, dark and slightly menacing, but shot through with that silken, suggestive thread of promise. That promise of pain and pleasure...and intense arousal. I'm shivering again, but this time it's not shock. There may be some fear there, some nervous anticipation certainly. But mostly, I'm shivering with sheer joyful excitement. He makes me feel so good, so vital, so alive.

"Ashley, answer me. Do you need to be punished?"

"Yes, yes, Sir, I do," I whisper my response as his lips explore my neck and throat, and I tilt my chin higher to allow him access.

"What should I do to you, do you think, Ashley? Should I whip you? Spank you? Maybe a punishment fuck? What do you think would work best?"

"I don't know?" I'm melting in his arms now. He can pretty much do whatever he likes to me as far as I'm concerned. Then, "What's a punishment fuck?"

"Ah yes," he murmurs, "not something I've ever been minded to try with you. You're always so hot, so responsive. You really wouldn't like a punishment fuck, my love, because I'd fuck you, long and hard, but I wouldn't let you come. You'd enjoy it, at first, up to a point, then the frustration would bite. You'll beg me to let you come, to touch you, to let you finish. But no, no orgasm for you. How would that be, do you think? Would it teach you respect?"

"How would you...? I mean, you couldn't... Could you?"

"Oh yes, I could. I definitely could. You know that. Do you want me to demonstrate?"

"*No!* I mean, no, please don't do that. Sir. Please..." My voice is trailing to a whimper, punishment fucking sounds frankly awful.

"Maybe we'll keep that for another time then, for a time when you really have earned it, for a time when you really, really piss me off. Today, I'm just mildly annoyed. I do think it's important to maintain a sense of perspective, don't you?"

My whispered "Yes" is perhaps a little hasty, but he takes it well, his low, sexy chuckle rippling along my throat as he gently nips and sucks my delicate skin.

"I think a whipping then, and I have just the thing. Very fitting for in here…"

I stumble forward as he releases me. I hadn't realized he'd been taking my weight. I lean against the barn door to support myself, turning to face him. He's silhouetted, caught in a strong beam of sunlight filtering through an open trap door above his head, his features completely obscured. He looks totally menacing. And totally gorgeous, a perfect example of male beauty, the powerful Dom and tender lover rolled in one. Just now though, powerful Dom is definitely in the ascendency.

He regards me for a few moments as I lean heavily against the door, breathing fast, my hand on my heart as it hitches up a gear or two. Then he turns sharply, strides away across the barn. Moments later he's back, a hard leather riding crop in his hand. He comes to stand in front of me, watching my reaction as he flicks the sharp leather tip against his hand. I can't take my eyes off it. I look at it, mesmerized, imagining the feel of it against my bottom. It will be my bottom, I'm sure of that. I imagine the hiss as it flies through the air, the sharp crack as it connects with my skin. My bottom clenches involuntarily, and my eyes are already starting to water.

Christ, that looks like it's going to hurt.

"Well, Ashley. Do you think this will do? Can I deliver a memorable lesson with this, do you think?"

"I—yes, Sir. I'm sure you can." I drag my eyes upwards to meet his steady green gaze, draw a deep breath. "Would you like me to get undressed?"

He considers for a few moments, then shakes his head. "No, not this time. I'd like you to bend over—that bale of hay over there will do I think, the same one we used last time—and lift your skirt. Are you wearing underwear, Ashley?"

"Yes, of course. Sir."

"Remove it please." He holds out his hand, expectant. I get the message and quickly pull off my knickers from under my long cotton skirt, hand them to him. He crunches them into a ball and shoves them into his jeans pocket. "I suspect you'll not be keen to put these back on when I've finished with you. Your arse is going to be very, very sore." And with that he turns and strides over to the bale of hay in question. He stops beside it, and beckons me to join him.

My gaze never leaves his as I make my way across the floor of the barn, before eventually standing beside him. He gestures that I am to bend over, lean on the hay. I do as I'm told, idly noting the pleasant, outdoorsy smell of the dry hay. It's tickly though, scratchy against my cheek as I lay my face flat on the level top of the bale.

"When you're ready, I'd like you to lift your skirt. I want it up around your waist, bunched out of the way. I'm not quite ready to start yet, but I do enjoy watching your lovely arse quivering before I punish you." He stops, stands back, waits.

And I know it's time.

My hands are shaking as I lift my skirt—the loose flowing cotton light and easy to pull up and gather in front of me—rolling it up into a loose ball of fabric which I tuck under me. My part in the preparations over, my bottom bared and ready and accepting of what's to come, I settle down to wait.

And, as usual, he makes me wait. He amuses himself for several minutes stroking the crop across my bottom, up the backs of my legs. He trails it down the valley between my buttocks, and as he reaches my anus I instinctively part my legs. He chuckles and continues to explore me with the hard, harsh leather. I remember the time he fucked me with the handle of a whip, once when I was really struggling to accept and tolerate a beating. And how that helped me, gave me ownership, a sort of mastery of my own. I don't feel in the least bit masterful now, and my breath hitches as he at last stops his little game and comes to stand behind me, the crop dangling loosely from his right hand. Now, he's ready.

"Ten strokes, I think. As usual, I'd like you to count them, please?"

"Yes, of course. Sir." And I stiffen, brace for the first one to fall.

I hear it momentarily before my right buttock explodes in pain. I hiss, the shock causing my back to arch. But I know better than to move. My hands are clenched in fists beside my face, my eyes are shut tight, my teeth grinding together. He won't mind if I cry out, he'd have gagged me if he wanted silence. But there's a little part of me that always worries in case someone hears, one of the Appleyards working late maybe, or coming back for something they've forgotten. No, best to be quiet. I don't want an audience. Not now, and definitely not later.

"One, Sir." My voice is remarkably steady, in my opinion.

The next stroke lands on my left buttock, and the effect is the same. I hiss, bite back a whimper, feel my nails digging into my palms as my fists tighten. "Two, Sir."

The crop falls again, this time landing on the back of my right thigh. The skin there is tender, sensitive, and I do cry out. "Th...three. Three, Sir." My tone is more ragged now, the pain starting to really bite.

The hiss as the crop flies again heralds the fourth stroke, perfectly positioned to land across my left thigh. This time I scream, not loud, not yet. But it's a definite scream.

"Four. Sir." I manage to grind out the number, then the next two as they land on the underside of my bottom, perfectly symmetrical.

My bottom, indeed my whole body, feels to be on fire, the pain rushing through me, filling every nook and cranny and tiny little corner, spilling out and sinking into the hay beneath me, trickling down through my bed of pain. My fists open, my fingers are now spread across the aromatic hay. I imagine myself, my whole being melting, flowing into the prickly bale. I'm weightless, formless, without substance. There's something I should be doing, something I need to think about, concentrate on. But it's gone, fluttering away from me. I jerk for some reason, moan softly, jerk again, then I'm still, floating, drifting aimlessly.

I can hear words, just faintly, distant, low and tender. I'm flying, lifting, moving. Gentle hands on my face, fingertips lightly tracing my features. Cool water trickling—a stream? A waterfall? Against my lips. Soft, refreshing. I swallow.

"Ashley, open your eyes, sweetheart. Time to come back now."

I moan, shake my head, sinking again. The cool water is against my lips once more, I lick, swallow.

"Ashley, you need to open your eyes for me. I need you to come back. Now." The voice is closer now, very close.

Command, instruction, I need to obey. I'm muttering, pleading, don't want to come out, not yet, not quite yet. But he's there, still there, pulling me, commanding me. And at last I obey. No choice, he's my Master. My eyes flutter open, and Tom's face is in front of me, he smiles, drops a kiss on my lips, still cool and wet from the water.

"Welcome back, babe."

"I— What happened? Where am I...?"

"In the barn at Greystones. I have you, you're safe."

"But I... What happened?"

"You went into subspace again. You were really down there this time. One moment screaming your head off, the next you'd gone. You're getting good at this, babe."

I'm struggling to sit up now, as the events of the last few minutes come rushing back. And wow, what events! I remember it all, perfectly clearly as the clouds shift. I recall Tom asking me to remove my underwear, then he told me to lay across the bale of hay. I have a vivid memory of lifting my skirt and holding still while he trailed the crop across my skin, making me wait. And the blinding pain, the searing agony as he laid the crop across my bottom and thighs, again and again, making me count the strokes. How many? It was to be ten, definitely ten. I counted five, or was it six?

"Did we, did we finish?"

"We did."

"But I was counting. I only counted to six..."

"I think it's fair to say you lost count, love. Lucky I was paying attention. I knew you'd stopped counting so I checked you to make sure you were okay. I could tell by your contented expression that you were happily floating in subspace, so I continued for a while."

"Oh, I'm sorry." I glance up at him, nervous suddenly. *Did I fail? Did I not carry out my instructions? Will there be consequences?*

My expression must have conveyed all my fears, because he laughs, gathers me in close and kisses my hair.

"You were brilliant, babe, absolutely stunning. Christ, you're so beautiful. I adore you, you know that don't you?"

I look at him. Stunned certainly, not entirely sure about stunning. He cups my chin, holds my face still for his kiss. His mouth is on mine and my lips part for him. He plunges his tongue in, deep, exploring, tasting me, loving me. And my arms are around his neck. I hang on, hold on for dear life as my world tips. Tom eases me backwards, across the bales of hay, settles me on my back. His mouth is still on mine as he reaches for the buttons on the front of my blouse, quickly slipping them open. My bra is a front fastening one, and he snaps that clasp too to release my breasts to the chill of the cool, shadowy barn.

His hands warm me, as he cups and lifts my breasts, gently at first, then more demanding. He circles my nipples with his fingers. They pebble and swell in the cool air, then he squeezes as the tender points harden, sharpening my response. Sensitive as always, my nipples are throbbing in his fingers. I moan into his mouth, gasping as he twists and pinches me, causing darts of pleasure and pain to shoot straight to my core.

Tom lifts his head, breaking the kiss. My sigh of disappointment doesn't last long as he fastens his mouth around my right nipple, suckling hard as he roughly disposes of my skirt, dropping it past my waist and down my legs. He lets it fall onto the floor of the barn, quickly lifting my upper body to pull my arms from the sleeves of my blouse. Naked at last, I lie under him, waiting for... Waiting for what? For sod all, that's what.

Suddenly gripped by an urge to be the aggressor here for once, I manage to get my arms up, my palms on his chest and push. He looks up at me in surprise, reluctantly relinquishing my left nipple which is now enjoying the same attention its twin just had. One enquiring eyebrow raised, he waits for some explanation of this rebellion.

"I want to be on top. It's my turn, let me be on top this time. Please."

Belatedly I remember the Dom/sub thing, but usually, by this point in proceedings, Tom's not too fussy about protocol. Sure enough, with a lazy smile, he rolls to his back alongside me. "Be my guest..." He folds his arms behind his head and closes his eyes.

And I get busy. Straddling him, I start by kissing his face, his cheeks, his chin, his neck. I kiss his eyelids, his nose, his mouth, work my way around to his ears, sliding my fingers through his hair. Satisfied with my explorations so far, I move south, opening his work shirt, gratified to find no T-shirt underneath. It is summer after all, and even up here in the wilds of Yorkshire the temperature does rise a degree or two.

I lick his nipples, small and hard, so unlike mine, but his reaction is not dissimilar to my own. He hisses, his mouth quirking in arousal, and I glow in the satisfaction of knowing I can affect him, as he can so easily arouse me. I move lower, unfastening his belt, then unbuttoning, unzipping his jeans. I start to pull them down, and he lifts his hips to help me. I hop down from the hay, drop to my knees to undo and pull off his boots, and his socks, before clambering back up to continue to deal with his jeans. My movements are stiff, my bottom still smarting from the crop, but I love the soreness. How far I've come on my journey to submission.

As I'm getting rid of the jeans, Tom leans forward, slips his arms from the sleeves of his shirt, and he's naked too. He lies back down, ready to let me continue. For now at least. And so I do, deciding to make hay while the sun shines. Or at least, fuck ourselves silly on it.

Tom's erection is nothing short of awesome. I lean back, my weight on my right elbow as I lift my head to admire it before reaching out, curling my fingers around the shaft. He's hard, a silken sheaf over a core of tempered steel. I explore, stroke, taking my timer as I allow my fingers to glide lightly up toward the head. Moisture is already gathering there, the drops of lubricant trickling from the small opening. I smear it around with the pad of my thumb, enjoying the creamy smoothness. I take him firmly now in my hand, pump the shaft sharply, and I'm rewarded as more moisture flows, dribbling over the head of his cock. Tom is moaning his appreciation, his cock jerking under my hand, perhaps as I so often jerk under his. I love the feeling of control, of power, the sense that for once he's mine to command and control. For now, he's mine. Mine to hold, to touch, to admire. Only mine.

Not only mine. There's someone else here.

I can feel it. I can feel eyes on me, on us. Not Tom's, his are shut as he lays himself open to my ministrations. But someone, someone else is close by. I'm sure of it. I stiffen, look around me. Nothing, no one, no movement, no sound. Nothing to betray any other presence. But still, I know, I'm sure. And I felt it when I first came into the barn, that unease, that prickle of — something not right. It's why I snapped at Tom, I was unnerved by it and at first blamed him. But I can feel it now.

Again I look around, and this time Tom notices.

"Something wrong, babe? Are you okay?"

"I, yes. No. I'm not sure. I just— I had a feeling someone was watching us…"

He smiles, lifts his hand to stroke my face. "There's no one here but us, babe, and maybe a few mice. I checked the place over before I texted you. If you heard something it's probably Chloe and her latest brood up in the loft."

"It's not, I didn't hear anything. I just felt…" I shake my head, smile at him, embarrassed now. "I'm sorry, it's just me and my over-active imagination. I guess I've not got over that messy business in Gloucester yet." Deliberately shoving the unease aside, I return my attention to his erection, still superb and looking extremely ready for action. This time I clamber up onto the hay bale alongside Tom and lay next to him, my face close to his cock and my body stretched in the opposite direction, my hips close to his shoulders.

"Now, where was I?"

His answering, "Yeah, sweetheart, you were just there…" is sufficient encouragement to hold my attention for the next little while. I take the shaft in my hand once more, tightening my fingers around it as I return to my work of pleasuring him. I've become quite adept over the months. I know exactly what he likes and I love to provide it when I get the chance. As often as not I'm tied up so opportunities to explore are fairly few and far between. I'm determined to make the most of this one.

I raise myself over him, hold his cock still, pointing straight up as I run the tip of my tongue around the head, tasting the juices there, loving the saltiness.

He moans, shifts under my hands, under my tongue. "Christ, Ashley, that's good. So fucking good…"

Stretching forward farther I take the head into my mouth and slide my tongue all around it, lapping at his saltiness, sucking slightly. His gasp of appreciation is all the extra encouragement I need, and I lean in further, take more. Reaching around I shove my hand under his thigh to stroke his balls. He thrusts upwards, and I take that as a signal my attentions are welcomed. I stroke his balls, cupping them to take their weight in my hand as he sometimes cups my breasts. I squeeze slightly, can feel the hard rocks held within the soft sack.

And suddenly, he moves. Taking my hips he lifts me quickly, placing my knees on either side of his shoulders, my smooth, swollen, sensitive pussy just above his face. I know what he's planning, but even so, the feel of the tip of his tongue lightly tracing my clit is so exquisite, so delicately elegant that I lose concentration for my task, all my senses focusing there. He uses his thumbs to gently, delicately part my folds, to open me as he slides his tongue inside. My head drops forward, my mouth slackening around him as I absorb the consummate perfection of his touch. Then my rhythm picks up again, matches his as he gently, sweetly, tongue-fucks me. I return the favor, moving my head to take his cock deep into my mouth, and I'm sucking with each thrust, sweeping my tongue across and around, loving the taste of him as much as I'm loving the feel of him, of his tongue on my swollen, sensitive clit. Then, just as my relaxation seems to be total, as I begin to suspect I might truly melt, dissolve into a sweet, smooth, puddle of pleasure just seeping into the hay, he slips his fingertip into my anus. And I go off like a fire cracker.

I moan, then shriek, really shriek around his cock, and I suspect he took his life in his hands—or more accurately my mouth—at that moment as I try hard not to bite him. It's touch and go—he touches and I go wild. My orgasm rushes at me, fills and consumes me, flinging me into orbit then spinning me around. Tom knows, knows what's happening, and increases the pressure. He slides his finger a little farther in, flicks my clit with his tongue just a little harder, before plunging the fingers of his other hand deep into my pussy again. I'm shuddering, enjoying the aftershocks as he takes my hips again and effortlessly lifts me, turning me to lie beside him. Then he's on top of me, his hips between my legs, his cock positioned at my entrance.

"Sorry, babe, it was you or me at that point. I want to come inside you, but you seemed so intent on what you were doing I needed to distract you. And it worked."

My only response is a satisfied sigh of welcome as he slides into me, swift, smooth, filling me to the hilt. He reaches back, hooks his arms under my knees to lift my legs, opening me more fully for him. It's perfect, so totally perfect, as he fucks me with such effortless skill. He angles his entry to enhance my pleasure—he knows exactly what, exactly where, exactly how. And within seconds it seems I'm spinning off into orgasmic orbit once more. I fling my arms behind my head, I'm gasping my appreciation, my gratitude as he brings me once more to a soul-deep, bone-rocking climax. I feel the waves of sensation flow through me, my body convulsing helplessly around his as he thrusts into me, deep, hard, fast. Unrelenting. And he's there with me this time, his own breathing catching as he at last finds his own release and his hot semen pumps into me, filling me, flowing within me. I squeeze, clenching hard, that semen even more welcome than ever given our new goal. I want to grab all of it, keep all of it.

Just as I want to keep all of Tom. Next time he asks me to marry him, he's mine.

A few minutes later we're both fully dressed again. Well, almost, Tom seems intent on hanging onto my knickers.

"You go on back, sweetheart. I just need to fill up the water troughs in the poultry run. I'll be along in a few minutes." He kisses me, winks and turns to go.

I slip out of the barn, letting the huge door swing shut behind me as I make my way back across the flagged yard to the main house. I'm halfway there when I feel it again, that prickle of unease, that sense that I'm not alone. I spin around, my eyes raking the barn behind me, the blank stone wall and closed door giving nothing away. My eyes scan the near area, the farther horizon. Nothing. Nothing to see, but still...

I shiver, turn and run for the house.

Chapter Eleven

Tom's more than a few minutes. It's a full half hour before he returns. And he's not a happy man.

"Someone's been living rough in the barn."

"What? How? Did you see him? There *was* someone there, I knew it…"

"Not anymore. But fairly recent I'd say. Loads of sweet wrappers thrown around, cigarette butts. Christ, lucky they didn't set the place alight. Dry hay and smoking don't mix. Cheeky bastards, I'd let them bloody camp there if they asked me. It's the ones who sneak in I can't stand."

I'm baffled. "What do you mean? Who camps in the barn?"

"Hikers usually. And not in the barn, well not as a rule. In the fields. I'm easy about it, it's not a problem as long as they respect the place, don't do any damage. But I can't do with people hanging around when I don't know they're there. Apart from anything else, I might shoot them by mistake. I've lost three chickens this week alone so there must be another fox out there and I'm looking out for the little bastard."

A fox. It was no fox I felt watching me. Some pervert, voyeuristic creep, just some sad lonely bastard getting his jollies from watching ours. And whatever Tom says about no one else being there, I'm convinced we had an audience today. And what a show we gave him! If Tom does shoot him, I for one won't weep. But I let it go. The only shred of comfort in all this is that it can't be Kenny. There's no way he's managed to follow us here, he has no idea at all where I live now.

* * * *

And now, it's early September. I stopped taking my pill nearly two months ago. My first period came right on schedule, but now, as of this morning, I'm an unprecedented ten days late. I'm optimistic, quietly confident.

I mentioned the possibility to Tom as soon as I suspected, as we'd agreed, as I'd promised. He smiled at me, crossed his fingers and offered to lick my clit for me, by way of celebration. I accepted his kind offer and spent the next hour or so spread out on the rug in front of the log burning stove, my knickers dangling from the back of the sofa and my skirt hitched up above my waist. My first orgasm burst forth readily enough with little or no real persuasion, the next two had to be coaxed from me. Tom slid a clit clip into place, and my engorged, sensitive little nub was helpless then under his skilled tongue and gentle teeth. And when he finally took the sensitive bud between his lips and sucked on it hard I screamed as I came apart. Only then, only after I was fully spent, did he slide his cock inside me and make sweet, gentle love to me, so achingly tender I felt tears brimming and trickling down my cheeks. I had never imagined, not ever, that life could be quite so good.

And this morning I'm just assembling my kit for a trip up onto the moors to replenish my 'Autumn Shades' portfolio when my phone tinkles. I wait a moment to enjoy my nice new ringtone—silver bells it's called, or something like that—before picking up the phone to see Eva's name there. I hit the green button. "Hi."

"Hi, yourself. Listen, I feel like some big girl company today. Are you planning anything special?"

"Not particularly. I was just going up above Top Withens to get some shots of the autumn colors appearing. It's good light today."

"Fancy some company? Me and Barney could both do with the fresh air."

"I'd love it. Shall I come over to Black Combe?" I was planning to call and pick up Barney anyway.

"No, makes more sense if we come over there. Quads is it?"

"Too right. Can you borrow Nathan's?"

"Already swiped the keys from his jacket. We'll see you in about half an hour. That okay?"

I can hear Tom's Land Rover outside, the engine note fading as he pulls up in the back yard. I smile to myself. "Tom just got back. That probably means I can sweet talk him into bacon butties or an omelet if you're interested."

"Interested? Do bears shit in the woods?"

"Not around here, as far as I know…but you're the professor."

"Ha ha. See you in ten." I hear the click, and turn to smile as Tom, flanked by jubilant, bouncing, border collie madness, comes through the door. He looks across the room at me, one eyebrow lifted in silent inquiry. I smile, show him my crossed fingers. He returns the gesture before coming over to me. He frames my face in his hands.

"Maybe it'll be as quick as this. Maybe not. But if not we'll just have to keep at it. It won't be easy, but maybe we should just pop back upstairs for an hour or so, for good measure..." His laughing eyes telegraph exactly what he has on his mind at this moment.

Pity I've just made other plans.

"Eva's on her way over. We're going out together today."

"Oh? Hitting the shops? A spot of clubbing maybe?"

"No. The moors. Pictures. You farmers might be able to take time off whenever you want to, to..."

"To fuck our lovely subs until they scream or faint? Whichever comes first." Always helpful, Tom supplies the missing words.

Even after all these months, he can still shock me into silence with his explicit, sexy, plain-speaking. I just stare at him, fumbling for an answer. "Er, yes..." Not the wittiest retort, on balance.

He laughs out loud at my obvious confusion. Prim little virgin I definitely am not, but even so...

"Right, well in that case you'll just have to wait until later. I guess you'll keep, and I'll put the nipple clamps back in the drawer and go find my pinny. Will you ladies be requiring bacon sandwiches today then?"

"Please. That'd be nice."

He just smiles over his shoulder as he lights the hob. Oh yes, Tom Shore can do 'nice' very well indeed.

* * * *

"Thanks, that was lovely. You know, Ashley, Tom's bacon was one of the first things I ever ate when I first came here." Eva turns to Tom, waggling the last of her sandwich in his direction. "And you still grow a good pig, if I may say so, Mr Shore." She shoves the last of her buttie into her mouth and swallows it before licking her fingers delicately.

Tom just shrugs, modest to the core. I don't think. "Most kind, Miss Byrne. More coffee?"

"Well, I don't know. There're no loos up on the tops…"

"Plenty of dry stone walls though, to nip behind." Tom's helpful advice is enough to convince Eva to hold out her mug for a refill.

Eva thanks him and turns to me again. "You know, Ashley, he really is very sweet. You need to hang onto him."

She's right, I do indeed.

"Maybe you could offer to have his children. That might work."

Tom and I exchange a look, an inquiry, 'Should we? And the answer, 'Yes'.

"She already did." Tom's tone is even, deadpan, the sort normally reserved for asking someone to pass the salt. Eva glances up sharply, looks from one to the other of us, obviously trying to work out what she's missing here. Eventually she turns to Tom, her tone equally casual, "Well, you should take her up on it then. It's the best offer you're likely to get."

"He already did." I put in my contribution, before Tom has a chance to answer for himself.

Eva's eyes are darting between us, working it through, then, "Oh! Oh. My. God. Are you…? Are you two…?"

I laugh. "It's early days, we're not sure yet. But maybe, we're hoping. Trying…"

With a screech of joy she's leaping across the table to hug first me, then Tom. Then Barney for good measure as he ambles over, attracted by the commotion. The collies ignore us totally, clearly too cool for all this malarkey in a morning. Eva's joy, in comparison, is quite unrestrained. "That's brilliant, absolutely brilliant. Wonderful. Congratulations. Does this mean you two are, well…long term? Or maybe, oh, I don't know…God. I'm babbling again. Can I tell Nathan? Can I text him now?"

"Yes, you can tell Nathan. That's all right, isn't it, Ashley?"

I nod, the silly grin plastered across my face in danger of becoming a permanent fixture.

"And yes, we're long term. And no, we're not getting married. I asked her and she turned me down. I might ask her again though, if I can get her in a good enough mood later." His wink at me indicating just how he thinks he might be able to bring about that happy state, and it's not lost on Eva either.

"Why did you turn him down? You must be mad. Didn't you taste that bacon? And I daresay he's okay in bed. Well, I wouldn't kick him out, though I expect Nathan would."

"Eva! There's more to consider than bacon butties and, and…"

"Hot, sweaty, satisfying sex, multiple orgasms, a six pack and decent pecs?"

We both turn to stare at Eva. I'm not sure which of us is most startled, but she just sits there, smiling at us over her coffee cup, a picture of guileless innocence.

"Miss Byrne, you shock me. That's not the sort of remark we normally associate with such a respected academic." Tom's dry tone belies the twinkle in his eyes as he reaches for more coffee.

"Have you been spying on us?" I glare at her sternly.

She shrugs, smiles sweetly at both of us before delivering her next killer blow. "Just a lucky guess. Well, why not marry him. He's not totally minging."

Tom's expression takes on a distinctly frostier air now, suggesting he's less than flattered by that assessment, but I do wonder if he might actually swallow his tonsils at her next remark.

"And he can manage a passable fuck by all accounts, and then a breakfast like this to follow. You could certainly do worse, Ashley."

Tom gapes at her, his eyes glittering now with what I so sincerely hope is mirth, but I'm not entirely convinced. I manage, with not inconsiderable effort, to keep my face straight, homing in on her initial question. "It's simple. He never asked me. Not really."

"I did." Tom dumps his coffee mug on the table with more force than usual, and has apparently recovered his powers of speech sufficiently to mount some sort of defense. He's not come up with much of a rebuttal, in my view however.

"No, you didn't. You offered to talk to my father. That's not the same thing."

"Ashley…" His warning tone is clear, the Dom asserting himself.

But now, I have a secret weapon, my hidden advantage. "Uh-uh, no spanking, right? And no whips. Your rules, and we agreed."

Eva's coffee shoots across the table as she coughs violently, gasping for breath. I reach out to pass her a cloth as Tom stands, moves around the table to pat her smartly on the back. Solicitous, he offers to fetch her asthma inhaler for her, but she manages to wave away his suggestion with a frantic flapping of her arm, her vocal chords still seemingly paralyzed. Satisfied her death is not imminent, he turns back to me.

"You two deserve one another. If you're going to talk dirty I'm out of here. Is Nathan around?"

"Yes, he's at home. In his office. Daniel's staying for a couple of days so they're planning a boy-fest—beer and football. That's why I'm over here borrowing Ashley." Eva's still gasping a little, a distinct wheeze detectable in her voice, but her coffee now seems to be all going down the right way again.

"Beer and football, that'll do me. I'm going over there then, so I'll tell them the good news and raid Grace's fridge since you two have eaten just about everything in sight. And, Ashley, you and I still have stuff to settle. With or without spanking. Given the prowess Eva seems so convinced I can drum up if pressed, I'm sure I'll come up with something suitably memorable by way of teaching you the lesson in respect you so clearly need right now. And I *am* going to have that conversation with Bajram." He nods politely to Eva, comes over to me, drops a light kiss onto my mouth and whistles for his dogs. "See you later, and take care out there. Have a lovely day, ladies."

Chapter Twelve

We pass Top Withens at a steady purr as we make our way up the moor, the warm late summer breeze whipping our hair around as we climb steadily toward my favorite spot, my viewpoint. I marked the exact patch of ground with a pile of stones and come back here every couple of weeks or so to capture and record the seasonal changes, the repainting of the landscape by fickle weather and shifting light. The footprints left by my tripod are etched in the bracken, like some sort of moorland crop circle, or lunar landing strip. This is my very own little bit of England. I've claimed it, staked out my territory, and I chart its journey faithfully. It's the same place, the exact same place, and different every time I come here. It takes my breath away, always stunning, almost airborne in its vastness, a terrifying beauty all its own.

I love to come here alone, but it's even better when there's someone to share it with. Barney's listened patiently enough as I've waxed lyrical over the months, and now it's Eva's turn. Soon, smiling to myself, it'll be the turn of my newest passenger, but

I'm still absorbing the reality of that, still not quite ready to let myself believe.

This is the place where I was when I spotted Rosie all those months ago now, stranded up on the moors. During those incredible few days when my life changed, almost in a moment. Days that started when I plunged to what, looking back, was probably my lowest point.

That was the moment when I was crouching, shivering and weeping on my frozen path trying to bury my beloved cat in the cold, hard earth. A small loss in the great scheme of things, but for me, then, it was the final straw. I'd nothing left, no reserves, nothing left within me that I could call on to pick myself up and carry on. Then Tom came. Out of nowhere, he picked me up, made me warm and took me with him. He took my side, refused to leave me on my own any longer, showed me what it was to be safe and cared for. Home, family, friends, work I love, a future I just want to grab with both hands.

Who knows what I might have achieved on my own, some of that certainly, but with Tom everything's just so much better. Tom's the sparkle, the laughter and the joy that fills my life. He's pleasure and pain and submission and glorious power all bundled up into one sensual, seductive package. And he's mine. I haven't agreed to marry him, not yet. But he's going to ask me again.

Maybe I can tell some of this to Eva, share with her. Not all of it, some things are just for me, or for us — me and Tom. But I do think this woman — my friend now, but so very different from me in so many ways — will recognize and share the intimate truths and sheer wonder of the lifestyle I've discovered.

Eva sits quietly on the heather as I spend the next half hour or so setting up my equipment, monitoring the light from various directions, assessing the most dramatic angles, planning my shots carefully. I'm toying with the idea of developing some 'concept' stuff, using digital painting techniques in Photoshop to drop new and bizarre elements into my landscapes. Images intended to amuse, intrigue, shock even. I'm wondering about some new wildlife for hereabouts, maybe a herd of African elephants ambling across the skyline, or penguins waddling along the tops of the dry stone walls. Or maybe some prehistoric images, dinosaurs perhaps, or a Neanderthal family squatting next to my quad bike. Or I could turn the whole thing into some sort of scorched earth, apocalypse scene, or maybe create a tsunami sweeping across the heather.

I mention my ideas to Eva, hesitant at first because after all, she may be a brilliant musician, but she's not known for her flair in the visual arts. The scientist in her might think I'm just plain absurd. But hey, she has a few ideas of her own, soon entering into the spirit of it. Being a scientist at heart she suggests images from space, alien technology, a Martian landscape complete with explorer rover vehicle. Or maybe we could slice through the hills and contours to show the geological layering beneath, the colors and swirling patterns laid down there over eons of natural erosion. We're really getting into it, our creative juices flowing freely as Barney ambles around, sniffing hopefully for any unsuspecting and unwise rabbits who might have strayed into our vicinity.

The shot when it rings out explodes around us. An instant of stunned silence, disbelief, confusion and a frantic yelp as Barney flies into the air then slams onto his side, blood oozing from a gaping wound in his massive shoulder. Eva leaps to her feet, we stand, bewildered momentarily, looking around for—what? An Irate farmer protecting his stock? A maniac waving a gun? A tribe of American Indians galloping on horseback across the moors. Momentarily I have a stupid, totally misplaced image of that as a digital painting before the awful reality hits me. Hits us both.

"Christ!"

"Shit!"

We both scream together, not sure who yelled what.

"Christ, some bastard's shot Barney." Eva leaps forward, heading for the stricken dog, now whimpering, his paws flailing as he tries in vain to get up. A second shot rings out, exploding the heather a couple of yards ahead of her.

"Get down!"

At my scream Eva throws herself down into the undergrowth. I crawl through the heather toward her, grateful that at this time the year it's fairly high, enough to give us some concealment. I reach her, and by common unspoken consent we're whispering. Sound carries for miles up here, depending on wind direction.

"He's aiming at us. Some bastard's taking pot shots at us!" Eva's frantic hiss reaches me as she tentatively raises her head. "Where the fuck is he?"

Another shot, and we both huddle deeper into our cover. We listen, the only sound now that of Barney's wheezing, labored breaths. He's no longer whimpering, and I dread what that might mean. *Oh, Christ. Oh holy fucking shit!*

Eva and I look at each other, both of us wide-eyed, horrified, terrified. Is it some mad trigger-happy farmer? Unlikely, Tom owns most of the land round here, it's his stock up on these moors. He wouldn't do this, neither would the Appleyards. Some idiotic kid's prank then? I doubt that too—the hole in Barney's shoulder wasn't made by an air gun. So what else makes any sense? Who else could it be? Only one answer springs to mind, and it's a scenario I can't bear to contemplate. Could it be that somehow he's found me again? Followed me here to finish what he started weeks ago in Gloucester? What I started two years ago in Bristol? With a dreadful sense of déjà vu, instinctively my hand slides across my stomach, my subconscious kicking in to protect the new life that I'm not even totally sure is there.

Eva rolls onto her back and wriggles around to wrestle her phone from the front pocket of her jeans. "I'm calling Nathan. And Tom. You dial nine-nine-nine." She mouths the words to me.

I nod, reach into the pocket of my hoodie for my trusty Samsung, praying either or both of us can get a signal up here. I can, and I bless O2 for their foresight and tenacity in sticking that mast on the slopes above Haworth, in spite of the objections of the conservationists down at the Rock and Heifer. Eva can't get signal—seems EE must have been fighting other battles.

"Which service do you require?" The disembodied voice sounds thunderous in the eerie silence.

I murmur my answer, "Police. Armed police. There's someone up here with a gun."

"One moment please." She sounds remarkably calm, maybe this sort of carry on is more commonplace than I thought. They do have some very strange ways here in Yorkshire.

"Police Emergency. Please can I take your name and phone number?" Another seriously laid back woman for me to talk to.

Panic mounting, I try to impress upon her the seriousness of our situation. Is no one listening? Maniac with a gun? Shooting at us?

But me losing the plot will get us nowhere. I bite back my mounting panic, my desperate fears for Barney, for Eva and me, and my baby, my utter confusion about what the hell's happening. I manage to tell the emergency services operator, quietly and with a degree of calm I consider nothing short of superlative in the circumstances, that someone with a gun has shot our dog, and is shooting at me and my friend. And just in case she still hasn't grasped the seriousness, I go on to explain that we're hiding in the heather on the moors above Haworth, the nearest proper road is five miles away, there's no cover apart from the heather for bloody miles, and we need help. Fast.

Still seemingly unruffled she asks me for the exact location, and as luck would have it I can rattle off an Ordnance Survey grid reference. This is my extensively documented and photographed little bit of England after all, I do know exactly where I am. She assures me help is on the way and asks me if I know who the shooter is.

I tell her I don't know for sure, haven't seen him. Her? But I think it might be, could be... I hesitate. If I say the words, it becomes real. My worst nightmare becomes my reality. As if to dispel any lingering doubt, any last remaining hope this might be just some bizarre mistake, some stupid misunderstanding, another shot explodes into the air around us, whistles over us as we huddle in the undergrowth, and shatters the tripod and camera a few yards away, the only landmark visible above the heather apart from our quads. But they're a couple of hundred yards away, too far to make a run for it, and in any case we'd be picked off as soon as we got on them.

I know the truth, no point trying to pretend this is all going to turn out okay. I stammer out my answer, "I think, I think it might be my ex-boyfriend. His name's Kenny Potts. He's known to the police in Bristol. He — he has a grudge against me, from when we split up, I..." God, it all sounds so sleazy, so bloody trivial.

"Was that another gunshot I heard just then?"

I'd forgotten the emergency services operator was on the line, could probably hear everything. "Yes," I whisper. "Please hurry."

"Help is on the way to you. Is there anywhere you can take cover?"

"No better than we already are. There's nowhere..." Another shot, and this time it's followed by a shout, a voice, one I recognize.

"The other slag can fuck off. It's just you I want. Stand up, Shaz." Kenny's voice, coming from somewhere above us, is still some distance away, but sound carries and can be deceptive out here.

"It's him, his voice. It *is* Kenny. Oh, Christ." I start to shake. My inner calm, such as it was, shattering now. He wants to kill me. I know he wants to kill me. And now, up here, all alone, he can. He really can, and he very probably will.

I lie still, my eyes closed, struggling to find some calm, some composure, some shred of resourcefulness buried deep within me. My life depends on it. So does Eva's, no matter what Kenny might be saying about letting her go. And so does my baby's life. And that's it, that's the key that unlocks my resolve, my determination to survive. Kenny killed one child of mine, he's not going to do it again. I'll see him dead first before I'll ever let him hurt my baby. He'll never get to hurt another child of mine.

"Shaz, you slag, can you hear me? You better fucking answer me or I'm offing the fucking pair of you. This is your last chance. Your mate can piss off, I don't give a fuck about her, but you're coming with me." Kenny's voice again, nearer now, definitely nearer.

We don't have much time before he's down here, flushing us out. I'm going to have to give myself up, take the chance that he *will* let Eva go and she can get down from here, let Tom and Nathan know what's happening, and bring help. They've got to be nearer than the police, and they know these moors. They can find us. Find me.

Then it occurs to me what I need to do, if I can. How to make sure Tom can find me.

"Keep still and keep your head down. I'm going to check on Barney," I whisper my intention to Eva.

"No, I'm closer. I'll go." And before I can protest, tell her to not do anything stupid, or at least if she does to be careful, she's on her way, slithering through the undergrowth like a commando.

"Get his collar," I whisper after her.

She halts briefly but doesn't turn, then she's out of sight, swallowed by the swaying stalks. I'm not sure if she's heard me.

"Are you all right, Miss McAllister?"

The operator's calm, disembodied voice reaches me again, penetrating the fog.

"Are you hit? Is your friend hit?"

"No, no we're fine. But he's still there. It's me he's after."

I hear a faint rustle behind me. Panicking I roll onto my stomach, sure he's found me but it's just Eva burrowing back through the swaying heather. A moment later she's back beside me.

"Barney's not dead. Unconscious though, he needs a vet and soon." She shoves his collar at me. "I got this. Are you thinking you might…?"

"Yes. It's the only way."

"Oh no, oh no you don't. That's a madman out there. A nutter with a gun for fuck's sake."

Yup, that's my take on this too. But I really can't see any other option.

I look at her, grasp her hand. "If he wanted me dead, and nothing else, he'd have shot me just then, not Barney. He had a clear shot, could have easily done it. He'd have been clean away. But he didn't. He's not going to kill me, or at least not yet. There's time for help to get here, for you to go and get help. Tom'll be able to find me with this." I take the collar from her, studying its length. Good thing Barney's so bloody huge.

She's frantically shaking her head, obviously never going to agree to this. Seems neither of us has any choice. Rolling once more onto my back I quickly pull the collar around my waist, pull the two ends together across my stomach. It's a tight fit, but it fastens. It can pass as a belt, more or less. I pull my the hem of my hoodie down over the top of the collar, make sure it's well hidden. Kenny won't even know it's there.

"Last fucking chance. You don't get away from me, not his time." Kenny's closer now, much closer. No time left to argue, to debate, to come up with anything better. Now, I give myself up and go with him.

"All right, all right. I'm here. Don't shoot, I'm here." With a last, desperate shushing gesture to Eva, and taking care not to make any sudden moves, I get to my feet.

Chapter Thirteen

He's there, maybe twenty or thirty meters away, a double barrel shotgun held stiffly in both his hands, its angry, hostile nose pointed straight at me.

"You fucking deceitful, treacherous little bitch." He lifts the gun.

I stop breathing. I stand, waiting for the shot, waiting for him to shoot me at point blank range. God, I made a mistake. A stupid mistake. What was I thinking? I should have listened to Eva, should have stayed down, stayed hidden. I had a chance then. Not much of a chance, but...

"Come over here, slag. Slowly."

Frozen, I can only stand there, rooted to the spot. The roar of the gun again jerks me into action as he fires over my head, then swiftly reloads.

"*Now!*" he screams at me, and I'm not sure in that moment which of us will lose it first. Him probably, I've got too much at stake now, and with that realization comes calm, a cool, objective detachment that impels me to think clearly, dispassionately, to treat this as just a film I'm watching, something happening to someone else.

With conscious effort I will my feet to move, to carry me forward, toward him, away from Eva.

His eyes are narrowed at me, bitterness and rage etched there. He hisses at me, malicious, hate-filled. "That's three times you've fucking left me, you tramp. Three times I've had to come looking for you. You're not fucking doing it again. You're mine. You've got responsibilities. To me. You owe me. I got three years 'cos of what you fucking did, what you fucking told the screws. And you're gonna fucking pay. Like that old bag paid, for interfering. For messing with me. You'll learn to do as you're fucking told from now on. And you'll learn what fucking happens to lying little sluts who can't keep their mouths shut."

He's ranting, incoherent. His eyes are blood shot, I can see that as I come closer to him. I wonder if he's drunk, but dismiss that quickly. No smell of alcohol, although he smells of just about everything else. His clothes are dirty, filthy, torn in several places, his skin weather beaten, his hair not washed in God knows how long. He's a mess, totally wrecked, looks as though he's been living rough, and probably has. His hands are shaking, and despite his accuracy in hitting Barney with one shot I'm wondering now if he really is that good with a gun. Maybe he just got lucky that first time.

The one thing that's absolutely beyond doubt, though — the one beacon of certainty in the whole of his rabid tirade — is his malevolence toward me. His hatred is there, palpable, obvious and undisguised. Malicious, bitter and eating him alive. My survival instinct is screaming at me now, telling me to calm him down, to do, say anything, whatever it takes to cool his rage.

I try the most obvious first. A groveling apology — "I'm sorry. I was scared, that's all. I was upset, not thinking straight. I'm here now."

"You're here because I fucking found you again. I had to come all the way up here to fuck knows where to bloody get you back. Again."

"I'm sorry, I..." My words are cut off as he backhands me across my jaw and I fly sideways, landing in a heap a few feet away from him.

He strides over to me and I know what's coming. I've been here before, many times. I instinctively curl around my stomach, protecting my baby as he kicks me in the ribs. I gasp, but manage not to cry out as I know from long experience that that will only enrage him even more. I've had years of practice at this, at surviving this. I keep my head down, lie still, wait for him to stop.

"Get up, bitch. Get up and start fucking walking." Again, that angry, hate-filled hiss.

I try to get to my feet, the pain in my side agonizing, every breath hurting and I know I have at least one broken rib. Not satisfied with my progress he grabs my hair and hauls me up. Now I do scream as he twists his hand viciously, and I'm sure my hair is coming out by the roots.

"Shut your sniveling mouth, you cheating, lying little cow."

He lifts his fist and I brace for the next blow, but instead he shoves me, hard, pushing me up the incline, farther from Eva.

This is what I want, to give Eva a chance to get away, to raise the alarm and get help. I stumble forward, cooperating but not too obviously. Every few yards he jabs me in the back with the shotgun, cursing me, promising retribution for all my crimes against him, imagined and otherwise. My mind spinning, desperately seeking an opportunity to escape, to tilt the balance back in my favor, however slightly, I shuffle forward. Uppermost in my mind, I'm trying to understand how the hell he came to be here. How could he have found me? He doesn't know this area, doesn't know anyone here.

My breathing is labored, painful. My ribcage is moving and shifting with every breath. Just one rib? Probably more. I can taste blood in my mouth, the inside of my cheek throbbing mercilessly. My right eye is swollen, closing. I try to calculate how long I might need to hold out, how long until Eva can get help and how long it might take Tom to find me.

Oh, God, what if he shoots Tom? He would, I know he would. Terror and despair start to build, threatening to overwhelm me, but the helpless presence of my baby grounds and steadies me. I *have* to survive, I just have to. It's that simple.

"Thought you could just grass on me and then fuck off and leave me, didn't you? Thought you could get one over on me, you and that interfering old bitch of a mother of yours. Well I taught her a lesson, showed her what happens if you mess with me. And you'll get yours soon enough, you lying little whore, same as she did." He's ranting, rambling, the words seem to be aimed at me, but he's not waiting for an answer, just babbling.

"Should have waited, waited for me, you should have been there waiting when I come out. Should have never put me in there in the first place, you slag. But you tried to fit me up and then you was going back with her, I knew it. Not fucking having that, saw to her good and proper. Stupid bitch. Interfering snooty old cow, looking down her nose at me like some bit of scum. Not good enough for her precious daughter, her little slag of a fucking daughter…"

I stumble, confused. He's babbling, right? He seems to be talking about my mother, but it makes no sense. He doesn't even know she's dead. How could he, I never told him?

"Got rid of the old bat, but I'm thinking I might keep you around a bit longer. Have some fun, eh?" He reaches for me, grabs my arm and spins me around to face him. "You were never up to all that much, frigid little cow, but you'll do for a quick shag…"

At last something penetrates. He's talking about raping me, but that's not what horrifies me. There's more, something much, much more dreadful here. I stagger backwards, staring at him, wide-eyed, appalled. "Got rid? What do you mean, 'got rid'?" An awful notion, something truly unthinkable, truly horrendous, is curling darkly around the back of my mind, an ugly suspicion, gathering form and taking root. My voice is a whisper, "What are you talking about? Who did you get rid of?"

"Your fucking mother, that's what I'm talking about. God, you're as stupid as her. Snooty cow, thought she could get one over on me. And you, you were just as fucking bad. Did the pair of you think I wouldn't know? Did you think I wouldn't work out that you grassed me up, got me put inside, and then you were planning to dump me again and piss off with her as soon as you got out? No way, not happening. Not fucking happening."

I dread the answer to my next question, but I have to know. "What did you do?" My voice is low now, controlled, as I ask what I need to ask.

"I got shut. Fucking got rid of her."

"She died in an accident, a hit and run…"

He laughs. Actually laughs in my face as he sneers at me. "An accident—yeah. An accident I arranged. An accident I fucking paid for. Except I didn't. I never even had to pay up. 'Cos Tony's fucking stupid too. Promised the stupid git five hundred quid to run her over, but the fucking moron never had the sense to get the cash up front."

My head's reeling, I'm still struggling to find a reason not to accept, not to believe what he's saying. It can't be true. It's just too awful, too cruel, too senseless even for Kenny. "Tony…?"

And now he's laughing, no doubt finding humor in my horrified expression, gloating, proud of his brutal solution to his problem. "Tony—Tony who shared a cell with me, got out two weeks before you were due to. Just enough time to nick a car and work out where to do the hit."

"Oh no, oh, Christ…" I drop to my knees, my face in my hands as the truth settles upon me like a dark cloud, crushing me. The cruel, bitter reality of a senseless, meaningless death. Of a life wiped out because some lowlife thug thought he'd found an easy way to earn a few hundred quid. Five hundred pounds for Christ's sake. Five hundred pounds was all it had cost to rob me of my family and my future.

"Fucking shut up, it was your fault. You did it, not me. You caused all of it. I've got rights, you owe me. You stay with me until I say you can go. Until I fucking say. And you never, ever, grass on me. Not fucking ever. You knew that, you fucking knew what I'd do, what'll happen to you now. What always happens to lying little shits who go crawling to the fucking cops." His voice is rising, he's bending over me, shouting the words into my face. His hatred and bitterness are all that's driving him, distorting everything in his head, twisting his reality.

I deliberately, forcefully shove my grief aside, try to tune in, try to listen, to understand what he's saying, how this all looks to him. Because if I'm getting out of this, if I'm going to be able to give myself any chance at all, it's going to be because I managed to get inside his head, managed to see which were the right buttons to press to calm him down. He's deluded, just plain crazy. Any moral compass he might once have possessed has now completely deserted him. I can't honestly recall a time when what Kenny Potts wanted was not exactly what *he* believed he should have. In his self-obsessed world he's the wronged party, the one owed an apology, entitled to retribution. That much is obvious, but it just makes him all the more dangerous, all the more unpredictable.

I try groveling again, forcing the words out when all I really want to do is throw up. "I know. I know that now. I'm sorry. I should never have..."

"No you fucking shouldn't have. And now you know what happens if you fucking cross me. If you grass on me? You can't get rid of me that easily. No fucking way. I got you back, got you to come back. Torched that flea-ridden house of yours and you came running back like a fucking stray dog. Stupid bitch."

I stumble, turn to gape at him. He stops, returns my stare, his grin malevolent, proud, as he enjoys my growing horror.

"So it *was* you. You set fire to my house." Even though we already knew, we'd worked out it must have been Kenny, it still shocks me to the core to hear him say it. Admit it. Gloat about it even. "But why? Why set fire to my house. I wasn't even there. But there *were* people in there, asleep. People could have been killed…"

He laughs, the sound a tinny cackle ugly, out of place here, intruding on the otherwise eerie stillness of the moors. "Serves 'em right, lazy fucking bastards. If they can't be arsed getting out of bed when the house is on fire they deserve what they get. Not my problem. I knew you wasn't there, I knocked earlier, asked for you and some spotty kid said no one called Shaz lived there. Said it was a student house, rented. So I thought if you'd rented it to fucking students you must have some cash by now. And you owe me. So I torched your fucking golden goose, see how long it took you to come running back. And it fucking worked, got you back there, that's all I wanted. And you fell for it, stupid cow. All I had to do was sit and wait, and you showed up. Like I say, you think you're so fucking clever, but you're as stupid as the rest. You and your fancy farmer and his ponsy mate with hair like a fucking girl."

I don't bother to point out that the 'farmer and his ponsy mate' took on six of them in Gloucester and came out without a scratch. Instead, "How do you know he's a farmer?"

He laughs again, the harsh sound now rasping in the wide open silence. I'm beginning to think he's ill as well as deranged.

"Cos I've been fucking watching you. Weeks now, I've been here, living up here. Been coming to your boyfriend's fancy little farm, slept in one of his barns for a while, nearly got caught by some nosy bastard poking around."

Seth Appleyard, probably. And suddenly I feel sick, remembering that afternoon in the barn, that feeling of being watched while we—Christ.

Sure enough, he's giggling, some sort of crazy childish cackling as he gloats over what he saw, what he watched. "Yeah, I've been watching you, and him. Pair of right fucking perverts you two are. I watched you fucking him in the hay, after he'd laid into you with a bloody stick. Maybe I'll do that, should have done it before. Might have taught you some fucking manners, could have taught you what happens to cheating little bitches who can't keep that shut."

Ha pauses in his tirade long enough to grab my face and jab at my mouth with the muzzle of the shotgun. I freeze, terrified, one slip and I'm without my face. I crumble, collapse in a heap when he finally lets go of me.

Leaning over me he snarls his hatred, "I was always too fucking soft with you. From what I've seen now you like it hard, you fucking love your bit of rough don't you? And that fucking farmer of yours is it, your rough bit on the side. I had to move out of the barn when that nosy bastard started snooping around, had to find somewhere else to live for a while. But I've been following you. And him. And helping myself to his stupid fucking hens when I felt like it. And more sometimes — you country folk really should lock your fucking doors once in a while. And be more careful about leaving keys around where anyone can frigging well help themselves."

I gasp, sickened. He's been in the house. *Our* house. And that day in the barn, he *was* there. He must have been well hidden because Tom looked around and couldn't find him. He found his left over rubbish though, knew someone had been there.

Tom used to leave a key outside for me. Under the log close to the back door. But he gave me my own key a few days after I moved in, and I've not seen the other spare key since. Why would I? I just assumed it stayed under the log in case of...well, in case. It sounds as though Kenny somehow found it, and from there on could come and go as he liked. I still can't believe that neither of us realized.

Kenny cackles again, obviously loving my horrified reaction. "And you hadn't a fucking clue, neither of you. I've been letting myself into your fucking house, helping myself to your food—nice bit of bacon, some crisps, sweets, whatever I fucking liked. I even slept there once. When you was away somewhere and the farmer pissed off with that mate of his, the one with the flashy car."

When I was in the Peak District? Tom did say he'd stayed at Black Combe one time, when he and Nathan had one of their football and beer fests. And all that night this piece of scum had been poking around in *our* home. Looking at *our* stuff, messing with *our* private things. Finding out about us, about our life. I'm not ashamed, not even embarrassed really. I'm an adult—I'll do what the fuck I like. But he's invaded me. Us. His unwanted, uninvited presence in our home has infected me somehow, left a dirty smear, and I just know I'm going to throw up. *Shit. Shit, shit, fucking shit.*

Oblivious to my reaction now, he goes on, wrapped up in his story, swelling with cocky pride at how clever he's been, how cunning, how ingenious to outwit us. "I've been up here, while you've been taking bloody pictures all day with that fancy camera. Nearly took it off you a few times, but you always had that fucking great dog with you. So I waited, waited till now, and I got a gun, your fucking farmer's gun, and I shot the bastard. Now I've got you. And now it's payback time, you dozy, cheating, lying little mare."

My head's reeling, trying to keep up, to take it all in. *Tom's gun? He has Tom's gun? But how?* Where did he get that from? I know Tom has a shotgun, I've seen it regularly. All farmers do, for dealing with foxes and other vermin. Tom's gun is properly licensed, locked in a secure cabinet in the farm kitchen, along with the cartridges. I've never used it, but I knew where it was kept. It seems Kenny did too. He must have taken it today, after we left the house. There's no way he could have broken into the gun cabinet and it not be noticed immediately.

I remember, Tom left first after our little heart to heart around the kitchen table, and Eva and I followed him out about twenty minutes later. I shiver, my revulsion now beyond any disguising. Kenny must have been there, watching, waiting for his chance. And as soon as he saw us all leave he must have let himself inside, broken into the gun cabinet and helped himself before following us up here. On the quads we made better time, that's why he was a good hour or so behind us. But he still had plenty of time, we were in no rush. So he picked his spot and got himself into position, then dealt with Barney. And more than ever I'm sure that was a lucky shot, but at point blank range, he wouldn't need much in the way of luck to murder me. He wouldn't even need a particularly steady hand.

He's still ranting on about my cameras and 'fancy fucking bike' but doesn't seem to realize that in his excitement about abducting me he forgot to also grab my expensive equipment. I viciously suppress the impulse to prick his self-satisfied bubble and instead decide to let that lie, I don't want him being seized with a sudden fit of greed and going back down there and maybe running into Eva again. I'm hoping she's got away, but I can't be sure. Instead, exhausted now and utterly devastated at the realization that he's been stalking me, spying on me and Tom for weeks, I rock backwards and forwards on my knees. My voice weak, I ask the one remaining question I can think of, "How did you manage to find me?"

He leers, obviously so damn proud of himself he's near to bursting with it. "Got your fucking address from your car. You left it parked in the street outside that fucking burned out house of yours when the stupid coppers come and slung you in their car—what a fucking laugh that was, but in the end they let you off. I just had to smash the window, had a look around, found a garage bill with your address on. Or his, didn't matter. I knew where to come looking for you, and here you are, you sneaking, lying little bitch. Here you are. And like I say, you're mine, you're not fucking off just when you feel like it. Not this time, never again. I'll always find you. And now you know what'll happen to you too, what happens to cheating little tramps who forget who's in charge, forget their place, tell the fucking cops about me and fucking piss me off."

His voice has risen, he's screaming into my face now, his eyes watering and the pupils dilated ominously, spittle spraying from his slack mouth. Christ, to think I once—even in my dim and distant and incredibly stupid past—ever, *ever* found this vile specimen the least bit desirable. The least little bit attractive. To think I broke my mum's heart for him. I gaze at him, incredulous. He ignores me, finishes his ranting tirade, "So from now on you treat me right, you fucking bitch, and you do as you're fucking well told. If I decide to take you back with me you'll never open that fucking lying trap of yours again. I'll nail it shut first."

I'm on my knees, dry-eyed but stunned, desperately trying to assimilate all of this, all of this crazy tale, this deranged series of events, the deluded, dangerous logic of Kenny Potts. And of one thing I'm absolutely certain—he'll kill me and anyone else who crosses him, gets in his way, without a second thought. What Kenny Potts wants—what he wants to do—is what he gets.

But I need to survive. I have a life to live. Two lives, if the one inside me counts too. I think it does, and I'll say anything, do anything, to get out us of this alive. So, more groveling... "Yes, I'm sorry. I will. I... What do you want me to do?"

He snarls at me, his hatred pouring off him. "Get up and get fucking moving. Not far now, then I'm gonna have me a bit of what's mine. A bit of what I've been missing out on while you've been dangling your bits in front of that fucking sheep shagging boyfriend of yours."

He jabs my shoulder with the shotgun, prodding me until I struggle awkwardly to my feet again. He means to rape me, that's clear. I tell myself I can handle that, if I have to. I survived that before, more than once. I can survive it again. Being alive's what matters, nothing else.

Except it *is* different now. Now I've had Tom, been with Tom, I know the difference. Kenny's self-obsessed, self-important, deranged ramblings are ludicrous in comparison to a real Dominant, a real Master. Tom commands me, Kenny just disgusts me.

"You thought I was stupid, thought I wouldn't see through that crap you told the police." He's behind me again, prodding me with the gun every few yards to keep me moving, keep me climbing upwards toward the highest crags.

I stiffen, grit my teeth against the pain as I struggle with the terrain. It's steep now, hard enough in good health but near enough impossible with broken ribs and one eye now completely shut. I wonder how long it's been since we left Eva. I've no notion of the time, no idea if she might have been able to get help by now, if anyone's coming, how much longer I've got before he decides he's finally done with me.

"You thought if you told the court I was with you those nights I'd not suss out that it was really you who told the fucking cops who did them shops. It had to be you, no one else knew. You were the only one who knew where the lock-up was. You thought if you said I was with you I'd think you was on my side, not know you'd double-crossed me. Not work out what you were planning, you and that evil old bitch. Not work out that you were going to dump me again as soon as I got locked up, planning to piss off with her. You thought I was fucking stupid, but it's you who's thick. I'm too frigging smart for you, remember that, cunt."

A wave of nausea washes over me. He knows. He really does know. He's worked it out. I did think I was being clever, but in reality all I was, was desperate. I covered my tracks as best I could but I couldn't break my ties completely. It was always going to come to this, if he found me. That's why I knew I had to leave, get away from my old home, try to start again somewhere else. And now, it's all for nothing. In his head I 'betrayed' him. He's bitter and vengeful and means to make me pay. The worst crime of all, the very worst thing imaginable in Kenny's criminal fraternity, is to be a grass.

He might, he just might have forgiven me for trying to end our relationship, settle the matter with a good battering and a few brutal fucks, but he'll never forgive me for telling the police. I can't at this moment really understand why I'm still alive now. He could have simply shot me back then. Whatever he says about taking me back, he'll never let this go. I need to get away, and soon, because unless I do, I'm as good as dead already. Like my mother.

My mind's racing, desperately re-assimilating, re-aligning what I know. Trying to make sense of it. One thing's glaring at me. And it chills me to my core. If he knows I was the informer—that it was me who turned in the ram raiding gang—then probably so do his mates who came with him to Gloucester that day. So, what was their motivation? Revenge maybe—that's what Tom thought. Or was it just the prospect of a bit of fun in the back of a van with a helpless girl? I shudder at the sheer idiotic cruelty of it, and at Kenny, who callously set me up to be gang-raped just because he thought he had a score to settle. Because he'd decided I deserved it.

Hugging my latest realization to me, I drop my head, stumble onwards, upwards, one step at a time, one foot in front of the other. I wrap my arms around myself in an attempt to ease my injured ribs, try to pick my way carefully across the now rocky uplands, clambering over granite boulders. One slip would mean a twisted or even broken ankle—no chance of escape then. There are no dry stone walls up here, the few sheep that venture this far have to pick out their own territory. They don't tend to stay that long, soon wandering back down to the lower hills. More shelter, more food.

"Over there, that way." Kenny gestures over to the right with the muzzle of the shotgun.

I turn in that direction, picking my route cautiously.

"There, between those two rocks. Get a fucking move on, we haven't got all day to piss about out here in the fucking cold."

I peer in front of me out of my one good eye, try to pick out where we are. There's some sort of cave ahead, just a narrow opening between the two rocks. I shuffle toward it, by no means eager to go in there with him, but still dangerously short of other options as long as he's waving that bloody gun around. I reach the rocky entrance, lean on one of the boulders and peer inside. Not quite a cave, the roof's not solid. The rocky floor inside is wet, there's water dripping down the walls. The place offers some shelter, some protection from the elements, from the wind maybe, but not that much.

"Inside. Now." Another jab in my ribs from Tom's shotgun has me groaning in pain.

I obey, scrambling across the threshold. Once inside, the first thing that hits me, overwhelms me, is the stink. The smell of the place is putrid, vile. It's clear this is the place where Kenny has been living rough since he was ousted from Tom's nice warm barn, and it's also clear he has no idea of even basic hygiene. One corner of his 'home' has been used as a toilet and the stench is appalling. My stomach heaves, I bend over and lose what little is left of this morning's bacon sandwiches. Not much, mercifully. I stand, doubled over, my hands on my knees, as I gasp for air.

"Over there, sit down and keep your fucking mouth shut for once else I'll shut it for you." He gestures toward the side of the 'cave' farthest from his crude latrine, where a filthy blanket is piled, along with a few old, damp newspapers and a green denim knapsack. A familiar green denim knapsack. He still has it, the same bag he made me pile the stuff in we stole from Tom. Christ, talk about life coming full circle.

Making every effort to breathe through my mouth, and only as little as possible, I shuffle over to the blanket and manage to lower myself to the ground, cradling my injured ribs as well as I can. Kenny busies himself, fiddling about with some lumps of wood, twigs and dried grass as he tries to make a fire. Luckily for us both, he's probably totally inept at it.

This 'den' of his is disgusting enough now, how much worse would it be full of acrid smoke from damp wood? He's crouching over the small pile of kindling, then he suddenly turns, lurches over to me. I flinch, cower away, but he just grabs the knapsack and pulls a small box of matches out. No doubt something else he stole from Greystones. Soon the tiny fire is burning, sputtering and pathetic, giving off minimal heat, but managing to fill the enclosed space with dense smoke. Coughing, I try to crawl nearer to the opening, desperate for fresh air.

"I told you to fucking sit down. Don't you move until I say so. I'll tell you when you can frigging well move."

Now where have I heard that before? The words are the same, more or less, but there the similarity ends. I smile to myself, struck by the irony, the utter and absolute contrast. The world of difference that exists between this deranged, pathetic bully waving a gun around, red-faced, screaming his threats at me, and the calm, commanding presence which is Tom Shore in Dom mode.

I roll back to my appointed place, lying down now to get below the smoke, to hopefully find some breathable air. Kenny continues to scuffle around, poking and prodding at his ridiculous little fire, dropping more pieces of wood and soggy twigs on it, generating more smoke and not much else. I'd have thought after all his practice in Gloucester he'd be at least a little bit better at fire-starting, but apparently not. He seems strangely and pathetically happy with it though, and soon stands, rubbing his hands over the tiny, crackling flames before turning and strolling across to his 'lavatory'. He opens his tatty blue jeans, and with a leer at me pulls out his cock—semi-erect, I note with some considerable revulsion—and he proceeds to take a pee. Shaking the drips off he doesn't bother to replace his tackle and zip himself up. Instead he turns to me, his cock dangling from his jeans and stiffening as I watch, my horror and revulsion apparently arousing him. He strolls arrogantly toward me, clearly proud of his manly display. And despite my best efforts I'm shrinking away, plastering myself against the rough stone at my back as he stands in front of me, his cock just inches from my face.

"Suck it, bitch. Suck me off."

I shake my head dumbly. Rape, I could handle. Maybe. But not this. No way can I manage this.

"Do it. Do as I fucking say." He steps closer, reaching for my hair.

I dive to my left, desperate now, ready to fight. He's faster and on his feet, so he has the advantage of height and weight. But I'm fighting for my life. He grabs my hair, hauls me roughly back, his fist raised to punch me again. I scream, and do the only thing that seems at all feasible, the only form of defense available to me. I savagely bury my revulsion at his disgusting display, and even more savagely I grab his balls. I grab them hard and I twist. Sharp, vicious, my fingers curled into his scrotum like claws.

The effect is instantaneous, and all I could have hoped for. Kenny's raised fist drops to his groin as he snarls his pain and rage. He is clawing at my hand as he tries to wrestle me off. But I tighten my grip, I have no alternative, the moment I let go I'm dead. It's that simple. So I hang on. I squeeze and I twist and I pull hard. He's raining blows on the back of my head and I block out all of that, block out everything except my death grip on Kenny's scraggy balls. He leaps backwards, away from me. Or tries to. I go with him, hanging on for grim death. Quite literally. He's almost dragging me across the floor of the grimy cave as each of us struggles for some sort of advantage. There's a sharp, searing pain across my thigh as I'm dragged into and across the sputtering fire, scattering the burning twigs. My leg's burnt, I know that, but I'll heal. And the fire is soon out, Kenny's little pile of kindling scattered across the cave floor. I know it's an unequal struggle, and eventually he'll win. And I'll most probably die. But not yet, not as long as I can...

My knee brushes something. Something hard and metallic that clatters along the floor as I catch it with my leg. It's the gun. Idiot that he is, he's only gone and left the gun on the floor. *Is it loaded? Did he reload?* I can't remember, and maybe he won't either. It's a chance, maybe. If I can just get my hands on it maybe I can...

"Armed police. Come out with your hands in the air."

The harsh, metallic voice echoes around us, reverberating through the cave, amplified by the rocks. No doubt borrowing strength from the adrenaline rush brought on now by sheer bloody desperation Kenny drops a last, vicious punch on the back of my neck and my world momentarily goes black as I collapse to the ground, my hold at last loosened. I can hear the voice, that huge, autocratic, compelling voice, barking instructions. I'm safe. They're here. I'm safe.

"Kenny Potts, you are surrounded. Come out now."

"Shut up. You fucking keep quiet. They can't find us, they don't know where we are. Can't see us in here." Kenny's muttering wildly looking around him for the gun.

He won't find it. Won't find it because I'm lying on it, hugging it to me. I chance a quick glance upwards, he's wheeling madly around in the small space, eyes darting around crazily as he tries to lay his hands on his weapon. Suddenly it dawns on him, he realizes where it is, where it must be, and he's back on me. He kicks me, hard, another rib, at least, gone. Then, with another obscene curse he lurches back across the cave and grabs for the knapsack. This time he pulls out a knife, and I idly note it's one I think I recognize, from the kitchen at Greystones. It's not a big one, not especially big. We use it for vegetables. But it's lethal for all that.

"Give me that fucking gun, bitch. Now. Or I'll cut you, I'll fucking cut you..." His voice has risen again, become a screech, an evil, malicious howl as rage completely takes over. Rage and desperation, and a deluded sense of self-preservation, still believing he can somehow fight his way out of this. He lurches at me, the knife now raised, his intention clear.

Now. It's my only chance, the only chance left if I'm to live. If my baby's to live. I grab the gun from underneath me and roll to my side, bring it up and point it at him.

The boom of the shot is deafening. Kenny flies back, flies away from me, splattered briefly against the far wall where only minutes earlier he stood and casually had a piss. Then, he collapses as though in slow motion, dropping down into his own filth.

Chapter Fourteen

I gape at him, writhing in the muck a few feet away from me, blood pouring from his shoulder. He's screaming, the sound splitting the air, echoing around us. Numb now, I drop the gun, sending it clattering away from me, horrified at what I've done. I scramble away, as far from him as I can in the tiny, confined space. I huddle into a ball, sobbing desperately.

"It's okay, you're safe now. Ashley, you're safe."

Tom. It's Tom's voice. And Tom's familiar wax jacket that's folded gently around my shoulders. "Come on, love, come with me. Let's get out of here."

Yes, out of here. I want to be outside. Numb, my mind a blank, I allow him to gently lead me out, to help me to my feet and half-carry me between the two massive rocks at the entrance into the brilliant light and fresh air. I'm aware of the two dark clothed figures leaning over Kenny, handling him roughly as they check for more weapons. They won't find any, he was unarmed. Unarmed, apart from a vegetable knife, and I shot him. I shot him at point blank range.

Outside, I sink to the ground again, and Tom lets me, lowering me gently. I close my eyes, my rasping breath harsh as I struggle to remain conscious in spite of the waves of pain now rolling mercilessly though my body.

"Paramedic. Get a paramedic here now." Tom's voice is raised, commanding and immediately obeyed.

No paramedics on hand, not yet, but two police officers are suddenly there, crouching beside me. Their appearance is terrifying, dressed all in black, their expressions capable, serious, implacable. But their hands are surprisingly gentle. In moments I'm injected with painkillers, their emergency first-aid administered swiftly, and soon I'm drifting in a strangely pleasant drugged haze, the pain in my ribs now just a dull ache. The euphoria doesn't last long though. I know what I've done. The police won't be gentle with me for long.

"I killed him. I shot him. Oh, Christ, Tom—I didn't mean to, he was going to... He was going to..."

"You didn't kill him, love."

"I did, you know I did. I had the gun, and he wanted it, and I..."

"You didn't kill him because he isn't dead. Not yet, anyway. He might be though, soon enough, if I get my hands on him." Tom's tone is firm, sure and certain. I try to take in what he's said, make sense of it. Not dead? Kenny's not dead?

Bewildered, I start to protest once more. "But I shot him..."

"Not you, love. Him." Tom gestures behind him, toward the entrance to Kenny's hideaway, where a tall, slim man, dressed in black with 'Police' emblazoned across his chest in large white letters, is just emerging from between the rocks. He has a large, deadly looking rifle in his hands. "Police marksman, nice enough chap, name of Terry. Had our friend there" — he nods back in the direction of the filthy cave — "had him in the cross hairs for a good couple of minutes before he pulled the trigger. He was warned, had a chance to give himself up. But he didn't, and he was about to stab you. So Terry had to stop him."

"But, it was me. I know it was me. I had the gun."

"You might have had the gun, love, but you didn't use it. You didn't have time to."

I lie still, my eyes closed, taking all this in. *Was it really not me? Is he really not dead? Kenny's alive...?*

"I would have. A moment later and I would have shot him. I know I would have, I meant to. I tried to." The certainty is there, in my voice. I know what I would have done. What I set out to do but mercifully someone beat me to it apparently. Tom clearly agrees.

"Meaning to, trying to, are not the same as doing it. You didn't, Terry did." He gestures again at the police marksman, now strolling calmly back to the police Land Rover as though shooting madmen on the moors is all in a day's work to him.

I suppose it is really.

Tom continues, "And he was aiming for the shoulder, so that's what he hit. He aimed to disable, not to kill. So Kenny'll live to tell the tale. He'll have his day in court. And our friend over there" — he jerks his thumb at the marksman, my savior — "he'll spend the next few days filling in forms and answering questions. There's a lot of paperwork involved in shooting tosspots, no end of bureaucracy. Terry won't be seeing his family any time soon either."

I look at the police marksman with even more sympathy — he saved my life, I have no doubt about it, and his actions prevented me from doing something I would have forever regretted despite the desperate circumstances, something I would have forever had to live with. It's a sobering thought, and I have a great deal to thank Terry for. I do sincerely hope his paperwork isn't too onerous.

Then, suddenly, Tom's other remark sinks in. *Day in court! Shit!* I grab Tom's arm. There's something I need to say, something important, vital. "Tom, he told me he killed my mother. He paid someone, someone called Tony, to run her over. It wasn't an accident. And he *did* set the fire, tried to burn down my house. He even admitted breaking into my car that day..."

"I know. We heard."

"What? How did you hear? Who heard?" Totally baffled, I'm shaking my head, painful though it is to move.

Tom reaches into the pocket of my hoodie and pulls out my phone, puts it to my ear. "Tell her you're okay, love."

"What? Tell who?"

"The police emergency operator. She's still on the line, been on the line the whole time, monitoring events. She patched the call through, we heard everything as we drove up here. A full confession. That'll be useful in court. And of course we knew exactly where you were—it was just a matter of how fast we could get here." He taps Barney's collar, my makeshift belt that led my rescuers straight to me. "That was quick thinking, love. Well done."

I remember the poor dog. Maybe there's still time to help him. "Barney. He shot Barney, we need to..."

"He's in the back of the Land Rover. Dan's working on him. It's bad, love, he lost a lot of blood, but he's got a chance."

A chance. I'll settle for that. Tom takes the phone, murmurs something into it, thanks the operator then ends the call just as the air ambulance buzzes over the rocky horizon.

In the event, it was Kenny who got to ride in the air ambulance. The lovely Jasmine Abbas, once more on duty and now seeming like an old friend, came over to explain that the helicopter only had room for two additional people. Even though he's only been hit in the shoulder Kenny was still the most seriously injured of the two of us, so they'd have to take him. I could go too, but I'd be sharing the small space with him. She shrugged, her expression sympathetic, regretful. Maybe I'd prefer…

She was embarrassed, but dead right. No way was I sharing any sort of space with Kenny Potts. Never again. So I went the long way round to the hospital, in a police Land Rover. Jasmine offered me more pain relief before we started our descent, to see me over the lumps and bumps of the moors in some sort of comfort, though she was reluctant to dose me with much given my likely pregnancy.

* * * *

I was in hospital for two nights while they strapped up my ribs and stabilized my pain relief. An obstetrician examined me, declared me definitely pregnant, and in no obvious danger of losing my baby as a result of my ordeal. That was the news I'd been waiting for, unable to think beyond the last time and how that all ended. When she left I smiled nicely, thanked her and turned my face into my pillow and cried.

And now, a fortnight later, Kenny is safely installed in the hospital wing at Armley jail in Leeds. His shoulder wound is on the mend, and I'm assured by Tom that Terry has finally completed the paperwork. Not so the police. They haven't come close to finalizing their list of charges yet, but it will definitely include murder, attempted murder, conspiracy to murder attempted rape, abduction and arson. There are lesser matters too, matters such as breaking entering, illegal discharging of a firearm, that sort of thing, but I expect the Crown Prosecution Service will eventually decide where they want to concentrate their efforts. Whatever, Kenny Potts is not going to be seeing the outside world for a long, long time. He's finally out of my life.

As for me, I've been back at Greystones for two weeks. I spent the first week in bed, alone most of the time, waited on hand and foot. Tom did most of the nursing duty, but Grace, Eva and even Rosie have all done their bit to coddle and care for me. They're all lovely. And they're driving me mad. I'm still confined to the house, just pottering about and getting thoroughly bored. Cabin fever is really setting in now, and as the bruises on my face have just about disappeared provided no one looks too closely, and my ribs only hurt when I laugh, I don't see why I shouldn't venture a bit farther afield. And I would, if it wasn't for the little matter of facing Tom afterwards. Even without recourse to spanking or whipping, his Dom persona is beyond stern about this and I know I won't be disobeying.

But I'm so bored!

I think back over the events of that day, the bits of it I didn't see but managed to piece together during the agonizing ride down the moors and afterwards in the hospital as Eva, Tom and Nathan filled in the blanks for me. Eva had stayed down, hidden in the heather until Kenny and I were out of sight and earshot. She told me she almost died when she heard the gunshot, that warning shot he fired over my head when I wasn't moving fast enough. And she heard the commotion as Kenny hit me, but couldn't do anything to help me, to stop him, nothing that wouldn't have just got us both killed. So instead, she did the only thing she could. She crawled back over to Barney to see how he was doing and kept out of sight, waiting until she heard us moving off.

She watched us shambling up the moors until we disappeared from view. Then she leaped up and ran for it. But only as far as the quads, still parked a couple of hundred yards away. She was on hers in a moment and roaring back down the fell, heading for Black Combe because even though Greystones was nearer she knew that Tom, Nathan and Daniel were at the house.

She was about halfway there when she saw the two Land Rovers coming toward her, up the moor, Tom's leading the way, followed by the police. She headed straight for them. Tom, Daniel and two members of the police armed response team were in Tom's Land Rover, Nathan was in the police vehicle with three more armed officers. They stopped to pick up Eva, and to hear her version of how events were unfolding as the convoy continued to head uphill.

I'd forgotten that Tom would be automatically notified of this incident, just as he was when Rosie was airlifted to hospital. As local mountain rescue coordinator, he's permanently on call, and of course the police contacted him immediately. They needed his local knowledge and a guide to help them locate the incident and find any casualties. He took the call on his mobile while he, Nathan and Dan were watching football at Black Combe, and of course knew straight away who was involved, what was happening. According to Daniel, both Tom and Nathan were ashen when they realized that Kenny was shooting at Eva and me, that we might have already been injured, or worse. All three of them were ready to head straight up the moors after us, but it was Grace who made them see sense, convinced them to wait for the police armed team to arrive, and join forces with them.

The police arrived at Black Combe about twenty minutes after Tom took that first call, and within another five minutes they were all on their way. The police had the Ordnance Survey grid reference that I gave to the emergency operator to go on as the point at which to start the search, and of course Tom knew the exact location of my viewpoint in any case. They also had a call out for a police helicopter to scan the area if required, though this would have been a last resort as Kenny would have been sure to see it and the situation could easily have escalated. And they had the conversation between Kenny and me on speaker in the police Land Rover the whole time as the operator was patching it through to them, so they had an idea what was happening, but not exactly where we were, where Kenny had taken me once we'd left Eva. Then Eva told them about Barney's collar, about how I'd taken it with me so they'd be able to track me. Nathan was straight on his mobile, phoned Grace who'd stayed at Black Combe with the children and got her to fire up his computer and locate the tracking device. From there she was able to give them my exact location, step by step, as Kenny and I made our way up to his hideout.

I'd felt so alone, so isolated, but in fact my rescuers were never very far behind me. The rescue team arrived at my viewpoint less than an hour after I left it with Kenny. They stopped there just long enough to pick up Barney, who was still alive when they reached him. It took Nathan, Tom and Daniel, as well as two of the police team to lift the huge dog and get him onto the flatbed at the back of Tom's Land Rover, but they managed it and Daniel got to work on him as they continued the journey up the fells.

It wasn't long after that before they had us in sight. Kenny and I had made slow progress, painfully slow, and the Land Rovers could have caught us up easily. As soon as they had us in view, the police were tracking us through binoculars. They could see that Kenny was still brandishing the gun, and of course they could hear our conversation so they knew just how dangerous and volatile the situation was. Even Tom, desperate though he was to reach me, and I suspect to get his hands on Kenny again, could see the wisdom in keeping their distance. So they left the vehicles out of sight and from there they tracked us on foot from a safe distance, until they could manage to close in without alerting Kenny. As soon as we disappeared into his 'cave' though, the rescue team were on us at a run, and within a couple of minutes they had the place surrounded.

Terry, the marksman who actually shot Kenny, crawled right up to the entrance and had him in his sights. He could have shot him, I gather, at any point as he was fussing with his little fire. They knew he'd put the gun down at that point so I was in no immediate danger. They were just deciding their next course of action when he started to lose it, started to attack me and I fought back. They issued their warning and Terry, stationed at the entrance, saw Kenny panic, saw him trying to get the gun from me. Then he saw him come after me with the knife, and that was that.

Bang.

Chapter Fifteen

And now, I'm bored! I'm going mad, I need to get out, go somewhere, do something. Tom has other ideas, at least about the going out. It's mid-morning, drizzling outside. Nathan, Eva, Rosie and a still heavily bandaged but more or less back to normal Barney, have just gone. Barney needed a good few blood transfusions, but being the size of a bear, the gunshot didn't hit anything too vital. He lost a lot of blood, but that was all — Dan managed to patch him up well enough working on the back of Tom's Land Rover until they got him to a vet. And now they're dropping Barney off to be cosseted by Grace while they're heading off on a shopping trip to Leeds, and I'm left here climbing the walls. Tom's been out on the farm since dawn and just wandered back in as the others were leaving. Apparently he's got a meeting scheduled for later on, but for the next few hours he's all mine. I guess things could be worse.

"Game of chess?" He winks at me as he rummages in the cupboard for the chess set. Having found what he's looking for, he leads the way into the sitting room where he opens the board up on the coffee table between the two settees, and starts to set up the pieces. I follow him in, stopping just inside the door to watch him. My beautiful man, all mine. He glances back at me, his smile warm, full of sensual promise. We do occasionally just play normal chess, but not often. I'm wondering what he has in mind.

"I got you a present."

Ah, interesting. A small square box is on the coffee table next to the chessboard. Tom shoves it toward me, gesturing that I should come and join him, take the settee opposite. I do and reach for the box. It's made of shiny red cardboard, quite plain, no clue as to its contents. *Could it be a piece of jewelry...?* Tom continues to set up the chessboard as I turn the box over in my hands. He's always giving me nice things—kittens, a home, a family. A baby. But not usually stuff you could gift wrap.

"What is it?" I tuck my legs under me on the settee as I shake the box.

Tom smiles, leans back to watch me. "It's your lesson in obedience. You recall I promised to explore alternative methods in view of your delicate condition."

I frown at him, puzzled. His expression is serious now, the Dom emerging, and my stomach is doing its usual clenching and churning as I anticipate some sensual feast. But not without some disciplinary action thrown in as my hors d'oeuvres it would appear, some form of enforcement to insure I know my place. Sexual submission requires continuous reinforcement, it seems. Cautiously I obey. I open the box.

Inside is a string of small silver colored metal beads, innocuous enough at first sight. I look up at Tom, puzzled. "What is it? A bracelet?" I pick up the beads, weigh them in my hand—look to him for confirmation.

"Anal beads, very sensual. You'll like these—eventually. For now though, be a good girl and go pop them in the freezer." He gestures toward the drinks fridge in the corner of the sitting room, the one he and Nathan like to keep well stocked with beer for their regular football fests.

My bottom clenches, my tiny entrance tightening defensively as his words sink in—as it becomes clear what punishment he has in mind for me today. I gaze at him, and one stern eyebrow lifts as he waits for me to obey him. I nod briefly and uncurl my legs.

Back on the settee, the beads safely ensconced in the ice making compartment of the fridge, I regard Tom warily.

He smiles pleasantly, holds out his two fists, a pawn clasped in each. "You choose."

I tap his right fist.

He opens it to reveal the white pawn. "Right, white goes first." He carefully rotates the board so the white pieces are at my end, and sits back. "You'll be wanting to get your beads back out of the freezer as quickly as you can, I daresay?" He lifts his eyebrow again, this time in polite inquiry.

I nod. "Yes, please, yes, I would." I know those beads are going to be inside me, and as far as I'm concerned the sooner the better. I'm relaxed enough about the general proposition, about letting him have my arse, he can do as he wants with it. It's all good, always. But I don't like it much when he puts cold things inside me and he damn well knows it. And he's using that intimate knowledge now. Icy penetration when I'm not expecting it is a shock, but to submit to it knowing what's coming? Now I suspect that's going to add a whole new dimension of excruciating to the ordeal. He promised me something memorable, and my Dom definitely knows his stuff. He's watching me carefully now, silent, but clearly waiting for something, his slight frown indicating displeasure.

I know that look, make the correct response. "I mean, yes, please, Sir." And I drop my eyes.

He nods at me politely, crisp and business like. "Right, the rules. You'll never manage to beat me, and definitely not feeling as nervous as you apparently do just now. You're trembling, Ashley. Are you cold already? Even before I slide those beads into you?"

I shake my head quickly. "No, I'm fine, thank you, Sir. Please, go on."

"The first time you manage to get me in check, I'll allow you to get undressed. And yes, I mean totally naked. I'll enjoy the view, I always do." He breaks off his explanation to rake me with his eyes, the gleam of lust clear.

And I know he intends to take his time over this — those beads are not coming out of the freezer any time soon.

With a smile, he continues, "The next time you get me in check I'll allow you to fetch the lube from the bathroom, and the next time I find myself in check, I'll allow you to apply it."

I stare at him, startled. This was unexpected. "Me? I have to do it?"

"Yes, you do. You'll manage very well I expect — lots of incentive. I'll watch, and when you've finished I'll be examining you carefully to make sure you're nice and — slick. And then, the next time you manage to get me in check, then you get to take the beads out of the freezer. You'll bring them here, to me, and then you'll lie across my knees and allow me to slip them inside you. You'll be quiet, the perfect submissive. You won't struggle or wriggle or offer any protest. You'll keep perfectly still and let me put them in, because if you move, or make a sound, you'll have to put the beads back in the freezer, and try to get me in check again. Then we try again. And we'll carry on trying until you finally submit, properly submit, or you safe word. Is that clear, Ashley?"

"I— Yes, Sir."

"Any questions?" His tone softens slightly as he says, "Any objections?"

I don't raise my eyes as I answer, just murmur my response, "No, Sir, no objections."

"Good. You start then."

I take a breath, and move my king's pawn forward two spaces. Tom nods his approval, and moves his knight first. We exchange moves, nothing spectacular, common enough opening gambits from both of us. Suddenly Tom makes an uncharacteristically unwise move, his castle shooting across the board to leave his king unguarded, offering me an opportunity to place him in check. He's done it on purpose, must have.

I glance sharply up at him as I slide my queen onto his back row. "Check."

He nods, smiles and leans back to watch me. "Stand here, in front of me." He indicates the spot directly between his legs. "Strip to the waist facing me, then turn around and remove the rest of your clothes. You can take your time, obviously. I'm in no hurry, although I realize you might be. Those beads have been in there a good ten minutes already, and you've still got a lot to do."

I stand, walk around the coffee table to stand on the spot he indicated. "You did that on purpose, you let me win."

"You haven't won, nowhere near. And you won't. But it's true I want you naked and I was fed up of waiting for you to achieve it on your own. The next bit won't be so easy. So, your clothes please, Ashley. In your own time."

He's right, I do have an interest in moving this along. I quickly unbutton my blouse and slide it off my shoulders. He holds out his hand to take it from me, carefully folding it before placing it beside him on the settee. My bra soon follows, to be placed neatly on top of the blouse. I raise my eyes, can see the appreciation in his gaze as he admires my breasts, now super sensitive due to my pregnancy. The bruising around my ribs has faded but the faint smudges are still visible. I see his eyes narrow as he notices and places his hands on my hips to pull me closer. He lightly traces the remaining marks with his fingertips, then with his lips before he lifts his head to take my left nipple in his mouth. He sucks softly, the pressure almost imperceptible, but still I shiver. He releases me, glances up into my face. "Still tender?"

I nod, my hand on his shoulder as with the other I frame his face, smile ruefully at him.

"If I hurt you, you're to tell me. Right? No suffering in silence."

"Right. Sir."

He kisses my bare stomach. "Turn around, drop the rest."

I obey swiftly, and soon I'm naked, his palms now smoothing the outer curves of my hips. "Your body is so beautiful, Ashley, so lovely..." He kisses the small of my back, the indent of my waist, as he reaches his hands around me to trail a soft path across my stomach and down to the apex of my thighs, the smooth mound there. "Open your legs, love, bend over for me." His command is whispered, but he expects obedience.

And gets it.

"Put your hands on the table. I'm going to make you come. Hard and fast. Do you understand?"

"Yes." I place my palms on the coffee table and spread my legs for him. I gasp as he parts my delicate, sensitive folds and he slips two, then three fingers inside me. He thrusts hard, twisting his hand to insure my inner walls are stretched, that the friction is intense. The sound of my juices flowing against his fingers just heightens the sensation, my wetness, my own heat. I moan, drenched in pleasure immediately. My knees shake as I feel the tightening of my inner muscles gripping him. He continues to finger fuck me as he reaches around me with his other hand to firmly rub my clit.

"You're so wet. Hot and wet and tight. Come for me, Ashley. Come now. Now."

"I, aagh…" It's over in moments. My orgasm grips me, I stagger under the onslaught, my hips pumping and gyrating furiously as the sensations seize me, overwhelm me. All my senses are centered on my core, and the wickedly delicious things he's doing to me with his fingers. It's only been seconds since he first touched me, and already I'm mindless with passion, dizzy, unsteady as the sensations crackle through me and out from my finger ends. I stiffen at the last, hold perfectly still suddenly as he takes over, holds me, carries me. Completes me.

The climax seems to go on, and on, and on, but eventually the feelings are stilled, the stimulation spent. He withdraws his fingers, once more kisses the small of my back. "That was good, Ashley. I'm impressed. You did well. You can sit down again now. It's my move, I think."

Still in something of a daze, I resume my seat and try to continue the game. He glances occasionally at me as he considers his moves. The play is unequal, I'll never beat him at chess. He's a master of this game as well as of me. We exchange moves, he takes a couple of my pawns, murmurs 'check' as he attacks my king, I parry, defend as best I can, until I suddenly spot another opening in the game. Another chance to place him in check. It'll cost me a knight, but I do it anyway. Time's not on my side.

Tom looks up at me, his slight nod and gesture with his eyes toward the door the only indication that I've passed the next part of my test. I stand quickly. Heedless of my nudity, I slip out of the room and head upstairs to find the tube of lubricant Tom usually leaves in the bathroom. It's there, in the cabinet. I grab it and rush back downstairs, place it on the coffee table next to the chessboard. Tom acknowledges it with a cursory glance and moves his king out of check.

The next few moves are unremarkable. Tom may have allowed me the two checks I've achieved so far, but he's clearly playing to win now. Forcing me to wait, to continue to play, all the time aware that the minutes are ticking past and those beads are slowly but surely freezing. My muscles tense defensively, the tight little opening squeezing shut in anticipation of the torment to come. I'm normally able to relax easily for this, allow Tom to penetrate me as he wishes, but I'm not sure this time. I'll try, certainly. I won't deliberately resist. But still...

"What are you thinking, Ashley. Tell me." Tom's tone is firm, not stern exactly, but he expects me to answer him. And to be honest.

Startled, I glance up at him, then drop my eyes again, stare at my hands. Then I answer. "I'm thinking I'm scared. Scared I won't be able to, you know, keep still and let you do it."

He pauses before responding, as though considering my concerns. "You know what'll happen if you struggle, if you try to resist?"

I cringe inwardly, dreading what's to come. Afraid I'll disappoint him, I want him to know I *will* try. "Yes. I won't do it on purpose though. But I just don't think I'll be able to help it. And then you'll make me put them back in there, in the freezer. It'll just get worse."

"I'll never punish you for something that's not your fault. You know that. Look at me, Ashley."

I raise my eyes, he holds my nervous gaze with his calm, green eyes, waits for me to steady. "And I'll never push you further than you can manage to go. You can do this. You will do it. Trust me. And after, I'll give you such a good time, babe. You'll feel so damned good, I promise you. Do we have a deal?"

I gaze at him, see the sincerity there, the generosity and the caring. All for me. A deal? Indeed so. I murmur my response. "Yes. Thank you. Thank you, Sir."

His eyes gesture once more toward the board. "Your move, love. Make it count."

I, too, focus once more on the game, consider the moves available. I reach out for my remaining knight, intending to close in on his queen. His sharp hiss stops me, warns me to think again, look again. I do, and see that I could move my bishop and put him in check for a third time. I glance sharply up, his eyes are smiling at me, his eyebrows raised. I smile my thanks and make the right move.

Tom nods, satisfied, and hands me the tube of lube.

I look at it, at him, back at the tube. "How should I...?"

"I want to watch, so I'd like you to kneel on the settee, facing away from me. You should be able to reach okay. You'll need to work it in well, inside as well as outside."

I continue to look at the tube in my hand, considering how best to manage this.

Tom's deadpan "Tick tock, tick tock" spurs me into action. Still another check to score before I can take those damn beads out of the freezer, no time to waste sitting around staring at tubes of lubricant. I unscrew the cap, and turn around on the settee. Oddly, I do feel embarrassed doing this in front of Tom. I've assumed the position and allowed him to work lube into my anus so many times now it should be second nature, but this is different. This is harder, much harder. Tom says nothing, just settles back to enjoy the show.

I squeeze a generous blob onto the fingers of my right hand, and reach carefully behind me to smear it over my anus. With a gulp, I gingerly insert one finger, just the tip, to test the opening there, try out the tension. The lube's good, my finger slides in easily. I stir it around, spread the stuff liberally before withdrawing my hand to reload. This time I try to put the lube just on my finger end, thinking to push it farther inside. I'm sure that the better I do this job, the easier my next ordeal will be. I intend to make a decent effort, and, determined, I continue my task. I press harder, push my finger farther inside, the first knuckle, then the second, gently pressing until it's fully inserted.

"Now two fingers. You need to make sure the entrance is open, ready for the beads. It'll be much easier for you."

I obey, heeding Tom's advice. I slide two lubricated fingers easily into place, and with my shoulder stretched and bent awkwardly to reach behind me I work them in and out, all the time acutely conscious of his gaze on me, watching this most intimate act, enjoying my humiliation, my submission to his will. Eventually, my fingers still buried deep within my bum, I look back at him, over my shoulder. "I think I'm ready. But would you check? Make sure I've done it right? Please?"

He gets to his feet, comes to stand behind me. I remove my fingers and drop my head onto my hands, kneeling in front of him, exposed and presented for his scrutiny. His approval. Wordlessly he pulls the cheeks of my bum apart, examines me with his eyes, then explores with his fingers. He's gentle, but firm. One finger, then a second, turning his hand to thoroughly explore my inner space. I groan, my clit twitching for attention in spite of my nerves, in spite of my humiliation. He knows, he knows how I'm feeling, is aware of my arousal and works it, builds it. I'm shifting, squirming, lifting my bum higher for him, silently pleading for another orgasm.

"Touch yourself if you want to. Use your other hand." His murmur is soft, the permission sweet.

I need no further urging and eagerly slide my fingers between my legs, rub my throbbing clit, soft at first, then hard, fast, the friction delicious as Tom continues to thrust his fingers in and out of my anus, his intention now clearly to arouse and satisfy. It works, it works quickly, and I climax again fast. My empty vagina clenches sharply, the ripples reaching his probing fingers. I hear his satisfied chuckle as he continues the inner massage and I finish my task, rubbing my fingertips furiously against my engorged, sensitive, greedy clit until the last surges of orgasm are pumped from me. Satiated at last, I relax. My fingers are still, although I'm still touching myself, tempted to slide them into my neglected vagina, see what I might achieve there.

Tom gently withdraws his fingers, pats the right cheek of my bum softly as he leans around me to pick up the tube of lubricant. "Hold still, I'm going to put more, directly inside."

I shiver as he slips the nozzle of the tube inside my entrance, now loose and receptive, and squeezes lightly. I feel the cool gel penetrate me, and Tom slides his finger gently in to smooth it all the way through. Business like, satisfied that I'm fully prepared, he withdraws, pats my bum again and steps away, returns to his settee on his side of the coffee table.

"Hopefully now you've had a bit of fun, you'll be able to concentrate on the game. You need to finish this, Ashley. And soon."

So the anticipation's getting to him too. Good. Maybe he'll help me again.

I turn around, acutely aware of the wetness, the lube oozing within and around me. I'm surely going to make a mess, ruin the settee. Tom grins, stands then leaves the room. He comes back a few moments later with a towel. He tosses it to me as he passes, on his way back to his seat. "Here, you might like to sit on that. Is it my move?"

I nod as I arrange the towel under my wet and very thoroughly prepared bottom. My words, when I manage to force them out, are remarkably calm, considering, "Yes. Yes I believe it is, Sir."

The next few minutes tick by slowly. We exchange moves, nothing spectacular. I lose my bishop, manage to threaten Tom's queen, he puts me in check, chases my king around the board for a few moves. I begin to panic a little. *What if this takes too long, what if my opening becomes tight again, closes up before he, before...* As ever, acutely attuned to me, Tom smiles at me, reassuring. "If you need to, if you ask me very politely, I'll allow you to prepare yourself one last time, just before you take the beads from the freezer. Will that help, do you think?"

My tight little smile back is answer enough, he nods, and we continue.

In silence we exchange a few more nondescript moves, then I see it. He must have done it on purpose, exposed his queen again. I can take it with my remaining knight *and* get him in check. It's a killer move. *Christ!* Has the invincible master of chess made a mistake? I look up, questioning. His green eyes are inscrutable, no clues there. He watches me as I look once more at the board, examine the pieces carefully for any chink in my plan, any sign I may be mistaken. No, it's there. I can do it, the move's legal.

Deliberately, I pick up my knight, catch his gaze once more, and place my piece carefully and purposefully on the same space as the black queen. "Check. Sir."

His smile is slow, satisfied. Full of promise and anticipation. And gentle, playful menace. "Well done, Ashley. So, do you want a moment to prepare yourself, or can we proceed?"

"A moment, please, Sir."

He nods, and I reach once more for the tube of lubricant. "May I?"

He nods. "Of course."

I turn on the settee, my back to him as before and lean forward. I take another generous helping of lube on my fingers and reach around again to place it where it needs to be. I'm relieved to find that my entrance is still receptive, still open. Without hesitation I work two fingers inside, taking comfort from the recollection that the anal beads are much smaller than the width of my two fingers. And Tom's fingers are even wider than mine, maybe he'll oblige me by shoving them in first, just to make sure. Maybe if I ask him nicely...

"It's time, Ashley. Go and get the beads." Tom's tone is all Dom. Stern, obedience expected. Immediate obedience.

I withdraw my fingers, place the tube of lubricant carefully back on the coffee table, the cap firmly screwed back on, and I get to my feet. Not entirely steady, I walk over to the drinks fridge and open the door. I slide open the ice making drawer. The pretty little beads are still nestled among the ice cubes, sparkling, shiny. And very very cold. Chewing hard on my bottom lip I pick them up, testing their temperature in my palm as I close my hand around them.

Christ, so cold. So bloody cold. I turn back to Tom, my hand curled tight around the beads, thinking to play for a bit of time to warm them up as much as I can in the few moments I have. A risky strategy, he won't tolerate much in the way of time wasting or prevarication, I know that. I make my way back to him, in no hurry, but not so much as to cause comment, attract further retribution. He has the lube in his hand, he's removed the cap again. He holds it out to me.

"Lube them up. Put plenty on, then place them there, on the table. He indicates the spot with a tilt of his head, then leans back to watch me do as he's instructed.

I manage to strike a balance of unhurried efficiency as I smear lube all over the beads, I count ten of them, graduating in size from one end of the thread to the other. They're heavier than I remembered, and very smooth. That should be helpful. There's a length of nylon cord extending from the narrow end and a small metal ring attached to the end of that. Obviously intended to facilitate easy removal. Idly, I note that the lube's warm, the coating will protect me. Maybe this won't be so bad after all.

A quick tilt of his head to indicate I should put the beads on the table now is all the reminder I get that Tom's waiting, and it's time. I put them down and stand awkwardly beside him, waiting for his next move. He places one foot—and I notice he still has his outdoor boots on—against the edge of the coffee table to push it away from him, hard up against the settee where I was sitting. He creates the space in front of him, and makes himself comfortable, his knees slightly apart. He looks up at me.

"You remember the rules? Once we start, you say nothing, make no sound. You don't move, or make a fuss. You don't wriggle, you don't try to resist. I mean it, and I could tie you up, or gag you if that might help. Would it, Ashley?"

I shake my head, quite definite about that. "No, I don't want to be gagged. Or tied up. I'll keep still. Well… I'll try. But…"

"That's good. You might want to safe word so a gag could be awkward." He pauses, watching me closely. "But what, Ashley?"

"What if it's been too long since I— Since I…got ready? What if I'm tight again? That'll hurt more, won't it?"

"I'll check before we start. Okay?"

I nod.

"Anything else?"

I shake my head this time.

He gestures to his thighs, his head tilted. "So...?" No further words, he drops his eyes to indicate I should lie across his knees. No detailed instructions required—I've been here many, many times before. I step forward, right up to him, place my hands on his left thigh as I lean over from the right, lower myself into position. I let go, allow my upper body to drape, to relax across and over him. He allows me the moments I need to shift and squirm and make myself comfortable.

"Okay, Ashley?" His voice is low, seductive. He's gently stroking and circling my buttocks with his fingers as he waits for me.

Despite everything the next few minutes are to bring, I do so love his touch on my body. He knows that, and he doesn't hurry, continues to caress me lightly. I stiffen, instinctively start to brace myself as he gently parts my buttocks to place a probing finger end in my slick opening.

"Ashley, you're tensing up. I know it's hard, but the more you can relax the easier and quicker this'll be. If you need a bit of time to collect yourself that's fine. But the beads go back in the freezer."

"No. Just do it. Please, do it now." I consciously relax my clenched buttocks.

Obligingly, Tom he wastes no further time in slipping one, then two lubricated fingers into me. He slides them fully in, thrusts several times to assure me that I'm accessible.

"Okay, that do you?"

"Yes." I hope he can't hear the catch in my voice. *Christ, I'm scared.*

Apparently not. "Yes what?"

Subdued, submissive, I give the desired response. "Yes, thank you. Sir."

He withdraws his fingers, and his body leans over mine as he reaches for the beads. This is it. I close my eyes, grit my teeth, absolutely determined not to disgrace myself, or even worse finish up with the beads back in the freezer and it all to do again. He gently parts my buttocks again, and I concentrate on slackening my muscles, on becoming as pliable as I consciously can.

And despite all of that, despite all my good intentions I jerk sharply as the first cold bead slips into me, it feels positively glacial and I hiss with the shock. I grip Tom's ankle, squeeze it hard, my hands shaking. He never said I couldn't touch him, and I hang on like grim death.

"I'll let that go, but no more moving. And not another sound, no sound at all. Understood?" His tone is hard, uncompromising.

I nod, uncertain if he can see me, but I don't dare speak. But he hasn't told me to let go of his ankle, so I hang onto it as the next bead enters me. And the next. Swallowing down my own sobs, catching them ruthlessly in my throat and choking on them, I force my body to remain still, rigid, as he gently but firmly slips the beads into me, one after the other. No hesitation, no cruel taunting. He just gets on, does it quickly. The intense cold burrows deeper and deeper, filling my core with its frigid, icy presence. I want to scream, I want to push myself up, push his hands away from me and grab the beads myself, or the nylon cord, and haul them out. But I just clench my fingers even more tightly around his ankle, bite down hard on the whimpers of pain surging from my throat as every fiber of my being screams for relief from the cruel, biting, freezing pain now filling me.

All I have to do is ask him. Just two words - Smithy's Forge - and it's all over. He'll stop, remove the beads immediately, no doubt hold me and comfort me until I stop crying. He'll tell me it's all fine, doesn't matter, because he loves me and he'll never hurt me, never really hurt me. Then he'll make love to me, and that'll be wonderful, tender and caring and generous. But I'm not going to ask, not say those words. Because I love him, he's my Master, my Dom, and I'll obey him if I can. I'll submit, surrender, trust him. And he's right, I *can* do this. I want to do this. For him, and for me.

"Lie still for a few minutes, get used to the feel of them inside you. Then I'll help you up, sweetheart."

The worst of my ordeal apparently over, Tom's voice is soft now, tender. I lie still across his thighs as his palm gently caresses my bottom. My teeth are chattering, whether from cold of fear I'm not entirely certain.

"Ready to get up now?"

I nod, murmur my response, and he slides his arm under me to gently raise my upper body, help me to straighten. I wince as the icy balls move inside me, the chill once more asserting itself. I bite my lip to keep from making any sound as he very gently turns me in his arms to seat me on his lap. He lifts the hair from my face, frames my cheeks in his palms. He kisses my forehead.

"You can speak now, love. And if you want to swear. I'll understand. Just this once."

Too miserable even for that I just shake my head, conscious now, for the first time, of the tears on my cheeks. It's been hard, so hard. The challenge of accepting, without making a sound, without moving, much more painful, in fact, than the icy chill of the beads. Even now, only moments later, my body heat has taken the edge off the cold. The beads are settled deep within me, with every movement they shift and roll, stimulating me in ways that are now both curious and erotic, an incredible sensation.

"You're crying, love. Your punishment's over so no more tears now. Please." And he's kissing my face, kissing my tears away. I lift my hand, stroke his cheek and his lips find mine. My mouth opens under his and his tongue reaches inside, probing, tasting, exploring. Mine tangles with his, and as we shift again, as he angles his head to deepen the kiss, the beads caress me internally. And it feels absolutely wonderful, the slight chill just adding to the sensation now as they roll against my sensitive inner walls, filling that forbidden inner space. He catches my startled gasp in his mouth, lifts his head to chuckle.

"I guess they're warming up?" He nudges my nose with his, playful, teasing.

"Oh, God, what's that...? How are they doing that? That feels... Oh, my." My head falls back as I moan my delight and pleasure. Tom takes the opportunity to reach down, between my legs, spread wide in instinctive invitation.

He tugs lightly on the cord and the balls jerk, shift again, rolling against each other and against me.

"Oh, sweet Christ..." I thrust my hips upwards.

He tugs again, this time drawing the cord across my clit.

I wriggle, frantic now, and he spreads his hand across my sensitive flesh, his middle finger just entering my anus. He presses on the balls there, at the same time using the pad of his thumb to rub my clit. I absolutely come apart in his arms, totally unravel as the sensation builds, explodes and overwhelms me. He increases the pressure, continues to stroke me even after the first frenzied climax starts to subside, and he whips it up again, now finding another finger to circle and tease the entrance to my vagina, dipping in there ever so slightly before taking my clit and rolling it between his finger and thumb. I'm writhing on his lap, and he gently lowers my upper body again so I'm lying down, my hair once more pooling on the floor as he brings his other hand into the action. I open my eyes, briefly glance up at him, but his eyes are no longer on me, on my face. Instead he's intent on watching what's happening between my widespread legs. He leans over, examining me closely as he teases and strokes me with his fingers, rubbing, easing me open, entering. He leaves the beads to do their job, to tantalize and torment me as he finger fucks me, hard and fast, his thumb never leaving my hungry, greedy clit. I shatter again, crying out now, frantic as the release claims me again, flings me around and spits me out to tumble, disoriented, back to earth.

As I start to calm, to recover some semblance of coherent thought, he glances back at me, smiles briefly before slipping both arms under me to lift me. He turns, places me on the settee and kneels on the floor in front of me. He positions me carefully, my bent knees toward him, as he slides his hands between them to push them apart. He spreads me wide again, angles his head to admire the cord still trailing from my anus, tugs it gently to get my full attention, then lowers his head. He nibbles his way along my inner thigh, first the right, then the left. He slides his palms under my bottom to lift me slightly, and trails the tip of his tongue around the lips of my pussy before dipping inside, tasting me. He lifts his head again, raises his eyes to catch mine, holds my gaze. I smile, tentative, fully satisfied already but still hoping there might be more.

There is. He smiles back at me, his gaze warm now, and tender.

"I love you. You are so beautiful, so very, very beautiful. Are you mine, Ashley? Are you really all mine?"

The wonder in his voice is almost my undoing. Is it possible to come just from words alone? Maybe. Maybe if I'd kept my mouth shut I'd have found out. But instead I respond.

"Yours, Master. All for you."

My reward? He dips his head and takes my clitoris once more between his lips, holding the engorged nub prisoner as he flicks it with his tongue, soft at first then hard as I rake his hair with my fingers, as I hold his head against me, thrusting my hips under his wicked mouth until I come again.

Long minutes later, he's lying beside me on the rug, naked too, leaning up on one elbow to smile gently into my eyes. I'm tired, but so, so happy. I reach for him, stroke his cheek with my fingertips, exploring the slightly abrasive contours there, wanting to feel, to know every part of this beloved face.

"I love you. God, the more you do to me, the more I love you. Is that normal?" I can't believe the way he makes me feel, the intensity—of pain and pleasure—and the bone-deep satiation of the aftermath. The now.

He smiles back at me, his eyes raking my body, as he lightly traces his fingers along my lines and contours.

"Normal? Who knows? All I know right now is I want to fuck you. Hard and fast at first, that's unavoidable. You're so hot and sexy and my balls are about to self-combust. You may not be able to keep up. But afterwards, it'll be long and slow and very, very thorough. Is that all right with you, babe?"

My smile is slow, sensual, welcoming. "Of course. How would you like me? For the hard, fast fuck?"

"On your knees. Turnover. Now."

I do, and with one hard thrust he fills me. I hear his "Fuck, baby, you're hot. So hot, and tight."

Then I can only feel as he pounds me, merciless, relentless as he pumps into me. He's not gentle, and the furious pounding causes the anal beads to spin and roll, the chaos of sensation once more exploding, ricocheting around my inner core. But he's right, I can't keep up. God knows how many orgasms have taken the edge of my desire, whilst his has been on hold, firmly reined in while he dealt with me. There's no reining in now as he climaxes, the hot gush of his orgasm filling me as he mutters his muffled curse of satisfaction, of male pleasure fulfilled and driven home. He leans over me, almost collapses on top of me, then he takes his weight on his arms, pushes himself up and swiftly withdraws.

"Now, on your back." His command is soft, murmured, accompanied by a light kisses feathering down my spine. I arch, sigh contentedly as I rearrange my limbs, ease my body over. He shifts, places his knees between mine, and I open my legs wide for him. He smiles at me as he positions himself at my entrance, his cock still hard, still ready. He lowers his head to kiss me, gently, but forcing my lips to part, to allow him access, a prelude to what's still to come. I can feel the tip of his penis slip between the lips of my pussy as his tongue plunges deep. He tongue fucks my mouth, leisurely, taking his time, as I gyrate under him, pressing forward, seeking more.

At last, he takes pity. He slides fully inside, hooking his arms under my knees to lift and open me even more. He penetrates me fully, his body stretching mine, the tip of his cock bumping against my cervix. I gasp my pleasure, my approval, my welcome, and he withdraws. Completely withdraws. Then he enters me again, does it all again, once more pulling out for the sheer pleasure of entering me again. I close my eyes, lie back, relaxed, totally accepting. He lowers his mouth to gently taste my nipple, and I moan, the aching sensitivity there, the fullness and tenderness induced by my pregnancy making me quiver with excitement as he so softly teases the tight, hard little bud. He turns his attention to the other nipple, careful not to hurt me, knowing my sensitivity there is exquisite to the point of painful. His mouth is on my neck, kissing me, tracing my jaw, the lobes of my ears. He releases my legs to lace his fingers between mine and draw my hands over my head. And taking his weight on his elbows, he thrusts, slow and deep. He angles his entry to hit my sensitive inner spot, attuned to my response as I gasp and sigh under him. This time we climb together, I squeeze, cling to him, tighten around him. He groans his appreciation, whispers to me that he loves me, and I manage to gasp out my own frenzied response.

"Yes, God, yes. I love you. Please, Tom, I need you to—oh, oh, God."

"Just 'Sir' will do, sweetheart. 'Master' if you insist."

"Just keep on fucking me like this and I'll call you anything you like…"

"Mmm, how about husband?"

My brain's fogged up, coherent thought eludes me. "What? What did you say?"

He chuckles, the sound low, sensuous, sexy. "It'll keep. Now cut the chat and squeeze my cock. Yes, like that."

I feel the familiar, irresistible churning and clenching as all my senses focus in on my inner core, where we're joined. I'm unsure where one of us ends and the other begins, and even less sure it matters. I start to climax, and Tom knows when I start to tip, increases the strength of his thrusts, his own pleasure mounting as he plunges hard. I grip him, desperate for more, more friction, more pressure, more stretching, yearning to be filled completely. I am, he does and we come together. He thrusts one last time, deep and hard, and holds the position as I quiver and convulse around him, the waves of pleasure washing over and through me. I feel once more the warmth of his semen on my cervix, and I cross my ankles behind his back to hold him within me, never wanting this moment to end.

Chapter Sixteen

Afterwards, apart at last but still entwined together, a lazy, satiated tangle of limbs, hair, sweaty bodies and mingled breath, Tom whispers in my ear, "I'm expecting visitors. In less than an hour. I need you to get dressed, love."

"Can't I stay here? You can just take them up to your office."

"No way. I want you to play the welcoming hostess. Not that this isn't a good look, but if you don't mind…?

"Welcoming hostess? Me? You must be desperate. Or just plain deluded."

"Desperate? Yes, sometimes. But you'll do for me, love. Now come on." He disengages, untangling his legs from mine, not without some regrets I'm pleased to note, and, agile as ever, gets to his feet. He leans down, offers me his hand.

I grab it and he hauls me up too. And with a pat on my bum, he directs me to the door.

"You've just got time for a shower. If you get a wiggle on."

I hear his groan as I disappear through the door, having just demonstrated the most sensuous wiggle I can muster.

* * * *

I'm in the bedroom, pulling on a clean white shirt to match my best burgundy trousers as I hear the car pulling into the yard. Tom's business meeting, and my chance to shine as his hostess. I've dressed for the part, not my usual jeans and T-shirt. Well, I should make some sort of effort.

Fully dressed now, I wander over to the window, lift the curtain to look out, get the measure of them before I have to go down and sparkle. I hear Tom behind me, following me to the window. He's been lounging on the bed, watching me dress, offering sartorial advice. He even helped me blow-dry my hair. I love it when he does that.

I'm puzzled to see not a taxi in the yard but Nathan's car, well, one of them. His business-like Sunday-best Audi rather than the usual Porsche is drawing sedately to a halt. I can just make out a figure in the passenger seat, and possibly someone sitting in the back as well. Difficult to be certain from this angle. Sure enough, Nathan gets out, and turns to open the rear door behind him. At the same time, the front passenger door opens and a man emerges. He seems vaguely familiar, I frown, looking more closely. He's not someone I recognize, as far as I know. He's tall, his hair very dark, like Nathan. But he's older, probably in his mid-forties.

I'm puzzled, turn to Tom, surprised to see Nathan in our front yard. "Why's Nathan driving them? I thought he was shopping in Leeds?"

"Nup. I asked him to pick up my visitors. From Manchester airport. He grumbles a lot but can be very accommodating when he tries."

I'm more and more at sea. "The airport? You sent Nathan to pick up your guests? Why not just let them get a taxi?"

Tom doesn't answer, just leans over me, watching as the stranger opens the other rear passenger door, and now two women are emerging to join him and Nathan in the yard. Much younger, little more than teenagers. In fact, they are teenagers. Surely they're not—they can't be business associates of Tom's. The man turns, looks at the house, then, maybe attracted by some movement in the upstairs window, looks straight up at us.

He smiles, slightly, tentatively perhaps. And our eyes meet. Eyes I've seen before. Seen every day of my life, in the mirror. Mute now, wonder dawning, I watch as Nathan also looks up, waves at us. Tom lifts a hand to return the salute, then takes my hand.

"Come on, love, we have visitors."

"It's him. Is it? Is it him?" I stand, rooted to the spot, staring at the man below me in the yard.

The two girls are now flanking him, also looking up at me, excited, their smiles broad. There are questions in their gaze but also uncertainty, as if they're not entirely sure of their welcome.

"Yes." Tom's answer is succinct. "He's my guest. And he's brought your little sisters. Let's go meet him. Them."

"You brought him here? For me. You found him, and then you brought him here. And my sisters too. All of them. They all came...?" I'm staring at him, disbelief etched all over my features.

He played it so cool. All day he knew. He knew they were on their way, going to be here soon, and apart from insisting I get dressed after he'd treated me to the most erotic experience imaginable, he never gave me a clue. Not a bloody clue.

He smiles at me, at my bewildered amazement. "Didn't take much persuading, love. They all want to see you, they want to get to know you." He cradles my face in his hands, kisses my startled mouth. "Let's go down."

I nod, and in a daze I follow Tom down the stairs. We arrive in the kitchen just as Nathan's opening the door, ushering our visitors inside. He doesn't follow them in though, just nods at both of us before slipping back outside and softly closing the door behind him. The five of us just stare at each other for a few moments, then...

"Sharon?" Bajram's deep voice, familiar, heavily accented, still insisting on putting the stress on the second syllable of my name.

He smiles, opens his arms, and I'm suddenly running. Running across the room to hurl myself at him. His arms close, folding around me as he holds me to him, pressed hard against his chest. He smells wonderful, faintly citrus and somehow exotic. And I'm conscious of other hands too, other people touching me, joining our hug. My sisters, all of them here, all here in my home. With me, with Tom.

And as if remembering his host at last, Bajram relaxes his hold on me, turns to offer his hand to Tom, who takes it and shakes warmly. The two men smile at each other, some silent understanding passing between them.

My father inclines his head politely to Tom. "Mr Shore, thank you so much for inviting us here. To your lovely home."

"It's Tom. And I'm glad you could come, sir. And so quickly. And your other beautiful daughters too. Welcome to Greystones."

He indicates that they should be seated, offers them tea. In no time we're all ranged around the kitchen table, smiling at each other as Tom fills the kettle. There's so much to say, so much to ask, to tell, and my head's full to overflowing. I'm wondering where to start. Bajram takes charge though, and, his expression suddenly serious, turns to Tom.

"Well, my friend. You asked me to come, and so I'm here. Now, tell me, what is this question you have for me, this matter you need to discuss with me which is of such great importance, this request that you couldn't make on the telephone?"

Epilogue

October 2013

It's almost a year to the day since I first came here, to Yorkshire. I sit, my feet tucked under me on the settee in the living room at Black Combe, thinking back over what can safely be described as a truly momentous year. Or I might be, would like to be, if I could only hear myself think.

All around me, deafening and drowning me, is the excited, rowdy chatter of a roomful of women. All the women I know, pretty much. Certainly all the women I love best. Eva, obviously. And Grace and Victoria. Rosie and Isabella, goes without saying. And my own sisters, Ayla and Melisa. Tom's mother is here too, the smart lawyer from Edinburgh. She's sweet, and seems to like me, thank goodness. And Abbie, my mentor in the fine art of submission, has made the trip across from York with her baby, five month old Michael Junior, the only male allowed in our little gathering this evening.

Even Summer's here. Summer, my generous friend from way back in Bristol, who let me use her laptop to download my very first images, and who let me chill at her flat, safe out of Kenny's way. I never went back to Bristol when I was released from prison so we lost touch. But I remembered her, and how much she helped me when I really needed it. I was virtually a stranger, but she was kind and generous, and I wanted to let her know how much I appreciated her. So I looked for her on Facebook, eventually tracked her down. I contacted her, asked if she remembered me, and if she did, would she like to come to my wedding. She replied immediately. Of course she remembered me, and she was delighted that I'd made good. She was surprised at the name-change, and yes, she'd be delighted to see me safely married to Someone Nice.

By some bizarre coincidence which I don't entirely understand, another guest is also a friend of Summer's. I only met Freya Stone myself a few days ago, when she and her partner—or more properly, Dom—a seriously intimidating man called Nick, came to Greystones to talk to Tom about a job for his teenage son. Nick is with Tom's party this evening while Freya chills with us. Nick's son, Callum, is now working for Tom at the farm. Both Freya and Summer know Dan, Nathan's brother. Small world.

But enough of them, because, this is my hen night. Tomorrow is my wedding day, mine and Tom's. He's having a similar bash over at Greystones—Nathan, Daniel, Bajram, Tom's father and three brothers, Seth Appleyard and at least two of his strapping lads. And Nick, Freya's partner—Dom, possibly, though I'm not entirely sure and I don't know her well enough to ask, and his son, Callum. They're all gearing up for a heavy session with beer and football. The drinks fridge in the lounge was stocked to overflowing before I left to come over here—there's every reason to suppose they'll be having a good time, although I gather they intend to make a raid on the Rock and Heifer later on. Apparently if Seth vouches for their good character, the landlord might let Nathan and Tom in. Or maybe, trade being what it is, the environmentally conscious innkeeper will make an exception to his normally fastidious entry requirements in view of the fact that twelve thirsty men, and one teenager, all inclined to invest heavily in liquid refreshment, can soften the heart of the most fervent of conservationists. Failing that, Bajram's quiet, persuasive charm should work on the landlady. It works on just about everyone else, even the normally haughty Victoria seems quite smitten. Eva thinks it's hilarious.

But back to me, because I'm getting married. Tomorrow. Imagine that!

In fairness, I'm not that bothered. I was happy with things as they were and wouldn't have rocked the boat. But Tom seems unexpectedly enthusiastic about embracing the married state. Who'd have thought he had such a traditional outlook? Bajram may have had a hand in forming his attitude, of course. He was drawn into our wedding plans when Tom requested his permission to marry me, that day he and my sisters first arrived, as we all sat around Tom's kitchen table. Since then he's taken a personal interest in driving the plan forward. His efforts gained new impetus when he learnt that I was pregnant. He and Tom exchanged words on that matter, not heated, but it was A Serious Talk.

My father insists on being at the wedding, and to be fair, I desperately want him to be there too, so it had to be arranged a bit smartish—he's due to return to Turkey next week.

So, we've raided Nathan's well-stocked wine cellar—well, outhouse to be more accurate—and I'm surrounded by happy feminine chatter as everyone tries to offer me advice on how to manage my domestic arrangements following the upcoming nuptials. I suspect the only advice worth hearing will be Eva's and Abbie's, and possibly Freya's, but I'm listening politely nonetheless. The less Tom's mother knows about our 'domestic arrangements' the better, I suspect.

I should be deliriously happy. I know that, and I'm trying. I'm really trying. I know how lucky I am, I have absolutely no illusions about that at all. But still, there's someone missing. Someone I want, more tonight than I have for many months now.

My mother—I wish she was here, wish she could see me now. I wish she could meet Tom, even more I wish she could meet her grandchild. But it's not to be, she's gone. Lost to me forever.

"Ashley, are you sad?" Rosie's innocent question somehow manages to permeate the din and chatter, falling like a party-pooping stone into the middle of our happy babble. Suddenly you could hear a pin drop, and all eyes are on me. I swipe away a tear, somehow manage to conjure up a watery smile, determined not to put a damper on proceedings.

"I'm fine, really. Really." I look around me at the anxious, caring faces, old friends, newer friends. And family too. And it's that family that now steps forward, in the form of Ayla, my sister.

Ayla's nineteen, and absolutely stunning. She's tall, slim, shoulder-length dark brown hair, thick and waving. Clever too—apparently she's something of a mathematician, like Eva. She's talking about transferring to a university in the UK to complete her degree, and Eva's using her influence to help make it happen. I hope it comes off—it'll be nice to have Ayla stay around a while. I suspect Isaac Appleyard, Seth's youngest son, won't be found weeping at the prospect either, but the less said about that around Bajram the better, probably.

Ayla's hand is on my arm, her soft, dark eyes smiling at me, warm, like her father's. My father's. "I have something for you. A wedding present. From your parents. My father asked me to give it to you if the moment seemed right. I think it might be good to give you the gift now. Yes?"

I look at her quizzically, tempted to correct the slight grammatical mistake, but what does it matter? I get her meaning. My father has asked her to pass on his wedding present. I nod, and thank her as she passes me a cardboard box. Not gift wrapped, it's a Turkish shoebox I think. Quite old, more than a bit dog eared around the corners and edges. The lid's been fixed more than once with Sellotape. I look at it, trying hard not to register my surprise. But this is not a toaster, I daresay.

"Open it," Eva urges me, perched on the arm of the settee alongside me.

"Yes, yes, Ashley. Open it. What's in it?" Rosie is desperate for a peek, is already poking at the lid, trying to lift up one corner.

"Rosie, be patient. It's Ashley's present." As ever, Grace's authority is absolute and Rosie subsides into restless bobbing about on the floor in front of me.

But to be fair, my curiosity is at around the same level as Rosie's so I don't hang about. With a puzzled glance at Ayla who clearly does know what's in there, I carefully lift the lid.

Letters.

Lots and lots of letters. In my mother's handwriting. Her letters to my father. Years and years' worth of letters. Collected over two decades, he's saved them all, every last one of her letters to him. I stare, dumbfounded, beyond surprised, beyond comprehension.

My mother's letters, her words, all here, all saved and now handed to me. Just when I most needed to hear her, she's here. With me. Forever. I thought she was gone, quite quite gone. I thought all I had left of her was her house. But she's back, her words, her thoughts, her private thoughts shared only with my father. And now shared with me.

I make no attempt to stem the tears streaming down my face, just lean forward to hug Ayla, sobbing into her shoulder. A little taken aback at first by this outpouring of emotion, she nevertheless rallies and returns the hug, and we're soon joined by Eva and Rosie.

It's maybe ten minutes before I'm collected enough to even contemplate starting to read any of the letters. Eventually though, I'm gazing into the box, wondering which envelope to pull out first. As ever, it seems, Ayla reads my mind.

"My father says they are in date order. And he's marked the ones he felt were most – significant." I look again, there must be a hundred or so individual envelopes all crammed into the shoebox. I rifle through, and see that some of the envelopes are marked with a red felt tip dot—obviously the ones my father thought I should read first. It'll take me a long time to read them all, but I will, every single word. For now though, I'll do as Bajram seems to be advising, and start at the beginning.

I look back at Ayla. "Have you read them? Do you know what's in here?"

"No. They were private, Susan's letters to my father. Your father. No one else but him has ever seen them. And now, he wants you to have them."

I nod, no further words necessary. I pull out the first envelope, the one at the top of the pile. I open the envelope and start to read.

Susan Spencer
11 Bridge Gardens
Gloucester
UK
15 January 1992

Dear Bajram,
Thank you for your letter, and for the photographs. It was kind of you to think of me and send them on. I miss Side, especially now when it's so cold here.

And of course, I miss you. I knew I would, but we would never have been happy, not forever. And it does need to be forever, you have to realize that. We'd both have to make such great sacrifices, it would wear us down, destroy our love eventually. You know I'm right. Please, tell me you know I'm right.

Aysin is your forever, not me. Your father was right, you belong there and I don't. I really, really don't. I belong here. So — I want you to be happy in your marriage, and in your life. Aysin is right for you, and you did love her. Before me. And after me too.

My life is here, and it's a good life. Especially now. There's something else I must tell you, even though it makes no difference to my decision. Our decision. But still, you need to know this.

We have a daughter. She was born two weeks ago, and is absolutely beautiful. I've decided to call her Sharon. She takes after you – see the photograph if you don't believe me. Her eyes are shut in that picture, but she has your deep brown eyes and your black hair. No English Rose, my little Sharon. But she's perfect, in every way.

Make no mistake, Bajram, I don't expect anything of you because of this. I'm fine, we're fine. My parents are delighted with Sharon, we'll be living with them. I have a good job, I can support myself and my baby and I'll understand if you don't want to be involved at all.

But if you do, if you want me to keep in touch, send you pictures, news as Sharon grows up, that sort of thing, just let me know. I'll be happy to keep in touch with you, but I don't want to cause any trouble in your future life.

Whatever happens, whatever you decide, please don't worry about me, about us. We'll be absolutely fine.

With love and all best wishes,

Susan

About the Author

Until 2010, Ashe was a director of a regeneration company before deciding there had to be more to life and leaving to pursue a lifetime goal of self-employment.

Ashe has been an avid reader of women's fiction for many years—erotic, historical, contemporary, fantasy, romance—you name it, as long as it's written by women, for women. Now, at last in control of her own time and working from her home in rural West Yorkshire, she has been able to realise her dream of writing erotic romance herself.

She draws on settings and anecdotes from her previous and current experience to lend colour, detail and realism to her plots and characters, but her stories of love, challenge, resilience and compassion are the conjurings of her own imagination. She loves to craft strong, enigmatic men and bright, sassy women to give them a hard time—in every sense of the word.

When she's not writing, Ashe's time is divided between her role as resident taxi driver for her teenage daughter, and caring for a menagerie of dogs, cats, rabbits, tortoises and a hamster.

Ashe Barker loves to hear from readers. You can find her contact information, website details and author profile page at http://www.totallybound.com.

Totally Bound Publishing

Made in the USA
San Bernardino, CA
11 October 2017